paternity

james calvin schaap

Other Fiction by James Calvin Schaap:

Home Fires
The Privacy of Storm (stories)
The Secrets of Barneveld Calvary (stories)
In the Silence There are Ghosts
Still Life (stories)
Romey's Place

paternity

james calvin schaap

QUIDDITY PRESS

Pine Valley, California

© 2001 by James Calvin Schaap

Published by Quiddity Press
P. O. Box 332, Pine Valley CA 91962-0332

Printed in the United States of America

All rights reserved. No part of this publication may be reproduced, stored in a retrieval system, or transmitted in any form or by any means—for example, electronic, photocopy, recording—without the prior written permission of the publisher. The only exception is brief quotations in printed reviews.

Library of Congress Control Number: 2001095469

ISBN: 0-9709623-2-0

For further information about Quiddity Press, visit our web site:
http://www.quidpress.com

First Edition

CONTENTS

PREFACE	2
INTRODUCTION	4
FALSE ALARM	8
THE VOICE OF THE BODY	18
EXODUS	36
PLAYING THROUGH	66
PATERNITY	82
WHAT HE NEEDED TO SAY	98
WHAT A MAN WOULD DO	120
FIRST BRIDE	146
VITAL SIGNS	174
CASA MIA	202
SCRIPTURE	232

PREFACE

Telling the truth...

The quality of recognizing the extraordinary in the ordinary; of being fully alive to the moment; of stripping down to plain thought all the confusions that layer us, that muffle the heart-cry within– this is the gift of the writer as prophet, the artist as writer.

Jim Schaap is much more than a courageous and compelling storyteller; he is a *truth-teller*. He creates life on the pages before us, cuts to the heart of it, and offers us, over and over, an old-new understanding of the varied ways of humanity . . . and of God.

Not a "good plot" . . . not religion, but *Truth*.

These vignettes are life lived out in all its joy and tenderness and grief and hard complexity. Some of it is rather harsh stuff; it's not prettified to meet a certain standard of purity. Happy endings are not a *given*. *Grace* is– in ways we always knew and never knew, in ways that unexpectedly satisfy. We want more– because here we have tasted the Real Thing. Here is *"love that will not let us go."*

This is a book for the young, and the not-so-young, for parents and those who struggle *with* them– for those who inhabit either side of the age-old chasm between fathers (and mothers) and their offspring. It is for those of us who wonder about this "foreigner" we thought we knew. Jim's "people" live it out– sometimes muddle it through. But always we walk along with them, cheering them on. And *that* is the secret weapon of a master storyteller.

Wherever you are in life, you are in these stories – or you know these folks well. Now you will know yourself, or them, just a little better. And love them better.

Judith Deem Dupree, Publisher
QUIDDITY PRESS

INTRODUCTION

More than fifteen years ago *Home Free*, my first novel, was accepted by a Christian publisher. The publisher's acceptance letter was, of course, a joy to receive, but their description of the novel rankled me. They said they wanted to publish the novel *because they were sure it would help bring healing to parent/child relationships.*

I was young then, full of visions and dreams, and I thought their admiration sadly indicative of an unstated evangelical aesthetic: "Fiction (art) isn't really good unless it's moralistic, unless it teaches somebody something 'pure'." I hadn't undertaken the writing of that novel with any intent of publishing a "how to" on parent/child relationships. I'd wanted only to tell a good story. I wasn't being moralistic; in fact, I was trying to be anything *but*. I was a Christian, but I was *doing art*.

A year or so later that novel served, in large part, as my academic dissertation at the University of Wisconsin-Milwaukee. The committee was composed of published novelists who made my day considerably easier than I expected by strongly commending the work. But late in the defense, one of them sat forward on his chair, tapped his finger on the manuscript, and looked up at me. "You know, Jim," he said, "reading this novel really gave me some insight into how to deal with my own son."

I recognized at that moment that some great chasm had been bridged. *Home Free* had done exactly what the evangelical publishers had hoped it would, but it did its work on someone who was supposed to be reading the manuscript as the *art* it was designed to be. Maybe it was "truth as art."

At that time I was reading the work of John Gardner, a man whose ideas about fiction were able to bring together the two worlds in which I lived.

In regard to fiction, Gardner uses the word *moral* in a fashion that makes both Christians and secularists cringe. He insists on the *moral* nature of fiction, that stories do have principled heft; but he is capable of upsetting evangelicals when he defines *moral* on his own terms, which have little to do with preaching about good or ill.

Gardner says stories provide guides to readers and viewers. The ones that stick to the soul become part of the compass by which each of us, as God-blessed decision-makers, judge between good or ill. Hamlet's reluctance to act decisively in the face of what appears to be treachery becomes, for us all, a possible way of doing things, a way we may or may not act ourselves. When, in stories, characters made wrong decisions, we observe that we do so too.

We learn about selfishness as well as unselfishness from stories; we learn both treachery and compassion. Furthermore, we learn where all these modeled paths of behavior lead. Stories provide models of behavior, Gardner says, in the same way that the life of Jesus, *as well as the life of Judas*, illustrates patterns of living for all human beings. In Gardner's sense the life of Judas, as a story, is as much a model of our being as the life of Jesus.

Flannery O'Connor said that a writer can choose what he or she writes about, but can't choose what she does well. We're all given certain predilections, certain gifts in our repertoires, which are not there because we've chosen them ourselves or even practiced them diligently.

Willa Cather told us that all of our best themes are already set in our childhoods. We don't really choose them at all. We'll never write about ideas that aren't set in us deeply as children– set there by forces much bigger than our own will.

What Cather and O'Connor assert may help to explain why I keep flailing away at fatherhood. I am a father; and the bulk of my worries in the last decade originate in the perplexity that simply comes with fatherhood. And I am a son, with a lot of experience on that end as well.

To dwell so substantially on one theme is frustrating, in a way. I don't come back to it again and again by my own design. I often wish I could take on larger issues of greater cultural significance– injustice, poverty, the clash of significant worldviews, post-modernity. But, for better or for worse, all politics is, for me, local. They're all in the family.

The stories in this book are what have accumulated in the last half-dozen years, outside of other novels and essays and a few plays. These stories emerge from experience and imagination, the synthesis of all stories, I suppose; and, whether I like it or not, they're all about paternity, about fatherhood, about parenthood.

For good and for ill, I guess, they're all models. By way of this collection, I hope some reader learns something about being on either end of the generational seesaw all of us, and these stories, ride. Somewhere in our individual pilgrimages, we're all part of that equation.

Soli Deo Gloria.

James Calvin Schaap
September 2001

False Alarm

When she came back from the clinic, she walked in the front door, stood for a moment on the throw rug, and leaned back with her shoulder to shut the door behind her, not once taking her eyes off him. He was a half-room away on the couch, where he'd been paging through the paper; but he was close enough to read what she meant to say when she shook her head.

They didn't really want a baby–that was the wrong way to say it, of course, but he didn't know exactly what to say just then because there was no hint joy on Shar's face, even though that morning when he'd left she'd been just as glum as she was now. But the answer was no. False alarm.

Something in him loosened. He let out a breath loud enough for her to hear and raised his eyebrows into a smile. False alarm. And then, finally, "It's good news," he said, in a tone so iffy she could pull it apart in any direction she wanted.

"I ought to be happy," she said, standing still. "I really am, too." Her jacket hung over her arm as if she had elsewhere to go.

"So am I," he said. "So am I, really." And then he did a good thing, he thought. He patted the couch beside him, urging her to sit.

"It's not like this happens all the time," she said. "And I'm no rookie either. Shoot, Mark, we've got three kids—are they home?"

"No," he said, reassuringly.

"It's not as if I'm stupid or anything—my word!"

"It's a good thing," he said. "You know it is."

She walked over to the chair across from him, where she sat, her coat in her lap, her eyes down on her twirling fingers. "I guess in a way I'd already convinced myself of the bad news, you know—I was sure."

He closed the paper in front of him and laid it aside, then sat forward on the couch, elbows on his knees, sifting through the right words from the rummage in his mind. "Shar," he said to get her attention, "Shar, it really is a big relief—you know it as well as I do. It's all for the best, you know—it's best for us, for pete's sake. All we needed was another kid at our age. I'm forty."

The moment it was out, it felt arrogant—my age, my life. "I mean, Shar—did you really look forward to redoing something into a baby's room?" he asked.

"New wallpaper, just picking out colors—"

"That'd get old real fast, honey. A basinet, a crib—"

"We got a crib," she said.

"That's for grandchildren."

"Mark, my goodness—April's still in high school."

"She's *already* there," he said. We're talking *caboose* of major proportions here."

"I know all that," she said, and she folded her hands together and bounced them on her knees. "I know all that, and I know this is by far the best." She looked at him again. "I'm old too. There are no guarantees anymore. You know what they say about old women—the odds of problems and all of that."

He tried hard to laugh. "Anyway, you know what Marv always says about tail-enders—how having Jeffie like that after so many years just about did him in. 'My friends visit colleges and I'm tagging along to kindergarten roundup. I'm old enough to be the kid's grandpa'—you remember that."

She toyed with the belt buckle on her coat.

"A half-dozen times at least I heard him say that about Jeffie—as if he were a curse."

"You realize what it would be like if things had turned out the other way." He raised his hand through the slant of afternoon sunshine from the south windows, swung it around as if he could clean up the particles of dust that hung, planet-like, in the bright trough of light. "You realize how hard you'd be bawling, Shar. Think about it. We'd be sitting here in each other's arms right now, wailing—no kidding, and you know it."

"I know it," she said.

"I'd be bawling myself," he said. "Another kid, shoot—"

She looked back down at her hands. He slapped the paper to the other end of the coffee table. Where were the kids? – he thought. The house never seemed so quiet.

He pulled himself to his feet and stepped out from behind the coffee table. When she didn't look up, he got the sense she wasn't to be touched just yet, so he turned away from her to look out the front windows. "Can you imagine another nine long months like the last time? Morning sickness, depression—big fat ankles. And how about a squashed bladder? Good night, Shar—babysitters again on weekends. Finding good ones." He tried hard to laugh. "We're free, honey. Another kid would have tied us up in knots. Crying jags—remember April's all nighters? I'll never forget the two of us in bed, lying there on razor blades waiting, finally, for her to stop crying."

He remembered the way she could sleep only on her back during those last months of pregnancy, her bloatedness, her mushroomed stomach, her horrible discomfort, varicose veins. "Bottles and baby food, all over again," he said.

Still, she said nothing. He pulled the shade back from the window on the front door and looked past the late afternoon shadow standing in a gray rectangle over the front lawn.

"It still feels empty, doesn't it?" he said, turning back to her. "Seems like there's a hole here, something missing–how come? What kind of feeling is it anyway that eats out your insides, when everything in my head says *no* is for the best for both of us?"

He walked up behind her. She was running her wedding ring up and down her finger. "Sometimes it felt almost like a miracle or something," he told her, "a big thing we never planned, something somebody laid in our lives, one thing that we didn't figure on–all of a sudden a baby. I mean, as far as I was concerned the whole family thing was over, and all of a sudden it seemed so outrageous to think that it could happen again." He laid his hands on her shoulders. "The silly kid felt like God's own hand in my life–like he just stuck his finger into our house when we didn't figure on him. Like a reminder or something – that kind of thing. You know what I'm saying?"

She reached up and touched his fingertips.

"It was as if God had said, 'This little thing here is just to let you know that I'm around,' you know? Just to let you know that I'm not tucked away in some steeple somewhere. So don't take me for granted, y'hear?' You know what I mean, Shar? It was almost the voice of God, almost."

"I heard a baby crying," she said. "I don't think it was God. I wouldn't want to blame him for what I'm feeling."

"Shar, we didn't want a baby," he said.

"We didn't?" she asked.

"No, sireee. We didn't. Just imagine how you'd be crying right now—just imagine."

"I'm half crying anyway," she said. "I am."

"It's for the best, and you know it."

"I know it's for the best," she said. "I know it in my head, but I can't get it straight in my heart."

He took his hands from her shoulders, put them in his pockets. "It's really unthinkable," he said. "Both of us up there in front of church baptizing a baby when we're old enough to be grandparents." He circled her chair and took a deep, audible breath before reaching for her hands. She laid her jacket neatly beside her, then reached for him, and stood, but he aimed her back to the couch, where they sat, together, his arm beneath hers, his arm over her stomach, her flat stomach. "It's much better this way, Shar—for us," he said. "You know that."

The shaft of light hit the beveled edge of glass on the coffee table and projected a burning rainbow against the north wall.

"It was like a bad dream," she said, "until today, until just now, until it wasn't there." She shook her head. "I don't know what's wrong with me."

"It's a kind of post-partum maybe—"

"How can you say that?" she snapped.

He shrugged his shoulders. "I didn't mean it bad, but there was something there, even if there was nothing there, you know?"

"How can there be something where there's nothing?"

"Well, if there was nothing, what are we crying for?"

"I'm not crying."

"I am," he said.

"You are not," she said.

"Inside."

She grabbed his hand in hers. "You feel it, too?" she said. "You feel as if something's been taken away?"

"It was always there, till now," he said. "I mean, this morning at school—I'm saying to myself that I can do it—if it turns out positive and we get a caboose, then I can do it. It's been done—that's what I'm telling myself. So it was there—the baby. The baby was there in my mind for the last week already. It's been done—I know it. Others have done it, so can I." He banged his hands down on her knee.

She squeezed his fingers. "We had too much time to think about it—some little yawning, pink-faced darling. I mean, he was already there in my heart, you know?"

"I kept seeing a girl," he said.

She snuck her left hand behind his back. "It's going to take some getting used to, I guess," she told him.

"I'd already conditioned myself for dirty diapers—all that yellow slimy stuff, and the smell, Shar—"

"Stinky ammonia smell all over the house, eating varnish off the bathroom woodwork—"

"We're up late every night—"

"What do you mean, *we?*"

"Okay, *you* up late every night."

"Sitting there in the old rocker," she said. "It needs paint, too. You'd have to paint it, Mark. For a new baby, I wouldn't rock in that thing anymore—"

"We're too old, Shar—"

"I know," she said.

"We're too old for a kid who never really was at all."

"I know that," she said again, and she brought both their hands to her face where what he felt seemed like silk. "You're so right, Mark. I've been telling myself every second since I left the clinic that it's all for the best. You haven't said one thing wrong—not a thing. You're so very, very right that it hurts."

He let it go, let it all fall into silence.

She took his hand and strung it around her shoulders, as if she were dancing, wrapped it over her and brought his fingers around to her lips, then kissed them, soft as first as a mother's touch on a wound. But when those lips tightened against his hand, when she held it there tightly against her face, he knew she was using him to block the tears pressed from her broken heart.

"I fell in love with a child that never was," she said.

He pulled her closer, nothing left for him to say. He pulled her closer wishing there was something he could do to cure it all, make it all right. But there was nothing more that could be said, nothing she hadn't already thought of herself.

And then, the shriek of the old back door opening.

Her shoulders straightened. She slid up on the couch and turned towards the kitchen, to the clatter of small feet up the back stairs, the sucking sound of the refrigerator opening, the smack of a plastic tumbler against the counter top, the splash of milk, the crumple of paper from an open bag of cookies.

The sounds of one of theirs coming home, he told himself, were right then the very words of the Lord.

The Voice Of The Body

Once our Brad hit high school, he took one look at his older sister, a senior honor student, and opted for a whole different course of study. Mary is bookish, tall and thin, and given to wearing plaid skirts of perfectly medium length. Every day of her high school career, she walked by herself to the bus stop or drove alone to school, and loved the quiet company of solitary mornings. Not once did we yell her out of bed or shoo her out the door. But from the first day of ninth grade, our Brad decided he'd have none of his sister's world. He set out on his own course, and if Ann and I would count the hours we spent wringing our hands about the boy we once wanted so badly, we'd tally enough time for a two-year leave-of-absence. But you don't take leaves from your kids.

He sat beside me this morning in church in much the same pose he always takes, slouching with his leg up against a hymnal, face down while he pushes back his cuticles with the edge of a dime. But I knew it was a pose designed to hide—maybe from me, or from himself, maybe even from God. This morning he was in church—I mean really there—even though we'd tugged him along for all the Sundays of his life.

Maybe it's a wonder it's taken this long. At eighteen, he's already a man.

Most anywhere south of here people would say most of the weather we've had this week is still winter. Early June isn't summer at all on the lakeshore. People wear jackets and keep their sweatshirt hoods up around their ears at the state park where Brad works. Damp gray haze lies so heavy along the shore that in the morning water beads on picnic tables all over the park, even though there may have been no rain. Sometimes a whole week of workdays can pass and you can't paint a thing with that kind of moisture. By calendar and climate, early June around here is really late spring. When the sun comes, it's a joy.

Brad was working in the booth at the park entrance Friday morning, maybe the first sunny day in two weeks of gloom. I know the job. Lots of things have changed around that park in the last twenty years—there's nature tours now, a new visitor center with wildlife displays, and the beach is finally coming back after too many years of high water. But some things haven't changed from when I worked my way through college down at the park twenty years ago. Somebody has to sell entrance stickers and register the campers. It was Brad's turn in the booth.

He told me he was outside when that Chevy van came through, an old wreck tugging a rack of Alumicraft canoes. He'd just grabbed a handful of camper receipts from the little box at the exit. There hadn't been much traffic into the park that morning, even though the blessed sun burned through the haze and likely pulled the soft blue-green from the long row of cedars I helped plant years ago down the road to the campground.

Brad let that conversion van into the park and the beach, sold them a daily sticker–two bucks. That was his part. All of it.

Ten kids from that van went out with two social workers, and four of them, delinquent kids from the city, went down, drowned in heavy surf not more than fifty feet off the beach. They made it out quite a ways, I guess, but two of them swamped and dumped, and four kids died. Two of those bodies were recovered that afternoon, and two stayed out, like ghosts floating in the swells.

I didn't know exactly what it was that Cecil told Brad until Brad himself told me last night on the beach. We live on the lake. Friday night I heard the front door slap shut, and when his cycle never popped, I assumed he went out to the water by himself.

Last night he took off again in silence, so I gave him fifteen minutes, and then went out myself and walked north towards the park because I realized he was probably looking for that last body.

The moon raised a sparkling triangle over whatever little waves hadn't yet bedded down for the night, and lights from the cottages down the beach stood in perfect order like a line of troops.

I found him about a quarter-mile down on the Sprigsby's dock, staring out toward the moon, his arm wound around a guy wire holding the runabout up above the water. The thin chill in the breeze off the lake kept your face cool and wet. "It's cold as April," I said, coming up from behind him.

"You out here?" he said, as if he hoped it might be someone else.

I walked past him over the planks and stood at the end looking out toward a necklace of lights from some ship. "I used to dream of someday standing here and seeing Michigan," I told him. "Just once in my life, I'd like to see land way beyond the blue." I turned towards him because I wanted to hear him say something, anything at all. "I think maybe if we'd get up on the roof of our place some night when things are really clear—maybe in a tree or something. Take some binocs along. Maybe we could pick something out." He shrugged his shoulders. "Ninety miles. Too much curve in the earth," he said. "You couldn't see over there even if it was crystal clear."

"Top of the power plant maybe?" I said.

He pulled the zipper of his jacket all the way up beneath his chin. "You could figure it out—how high you'd have to be."

"When I was a kid I used to think you could see it when you'd see these long lines on the horizon, like sand dunes—"

"Probably fog banks," he said.

I turned back to the horizon. The barge lights hadn't moved. "It's only a dream," I told him.

Somewhere down the beach a heavy bass from a party beat through the stillness of Saturday night.

He shifted awkwardly. "They found another one today."

"Where'd it come up?"

"Fifteen miles down," he said, pointing down the shoreline towards the lights from Port Jefferson. "It gets battered up, I guess. You wouldn't think it would, not rolling in the water.

"So one of them's out there yet," I said. "It could turn up miles from here." We hadn't really talked much about what happened. Brad doesn't really talk much at all to us anymore. Ann says since he's turned sixteen his only mode is silence, interrupted by an occasional grunt.

"Guess so," he said.

I didn't know then what exactly what was going on. I didn't know what Cecil had told him. He's young. Eighteen is too young for all of that, but I guess you think that way when it's your own you're worried about. "You blaming yourself somehow, Brad?" I said.

"Somebody's got to take it," he said. "Four of them dead. It's somebody's fault. I sold them a sticker. I let them in."

I tried to laugh just to lighten things. "You're taking the whole weight of the world on your shoulders," I told him. "You'll strain something if you try to do that."

"Cecil told me it was my fault." I couldn't believe it. "What do you mean?"

"He said I should have known better. I was born here, he told me. I should have known you can't take a canoe out into those waves—that's what he said."

I know Cecil's a fine man, an old warhorse from Korea who worked himself up to Park Director by sweat and loyalty and a powerful love for the lakeshore. He gave me a job years ago, and when I asked him about Brad last summer, he never hesitated.

"Cecil said that?" I said.

He twanged the guy wires as if they were the strings of a bass viola. "He's full of crap," Brad said. "It's not my job to be a lifeguard. I only sold them a sticker. He can't blame me."

Sprigsbys have a canopy on that deck, so they don't keep a tarp over the boat. We know them well. For some reason, Brad swung himself inside and sat down behind the driver's seat.

"We all need to blame somebody," I told him.

"It wasn't my fault."

"He doesn't blame you either."

"You should have seen his eyes," Brad said. "You ever see Cecil mad?"

"I used to work for him myself."

"He was mad. He read me out down at the booth, comes limping down from the office like he does, and just about tears my throat out."

"He didn't mean it," I said.

"The heck he didn't."

I know why Cecil did it. I know Cecil. He comes into the bank two or three times a week, deposits the take from the stickers and registrations. He's a fine man, but a dozen TV cameras all over the beach and all those reporters poking mikes at him, asking him how on earth four kids could drown in a well-maintained state park, and I can see him standing there speechless, a man who works with his hands but never was a talker. Besides that, right there at his feet are the bodies of two boys drowned in his park.

"It wasn't my fault at all, and he had no right to chew my butt the way he did," Brad said.

I turned around and walked to the side of the boat. "Then why do you think it is?" I said.

"I don't," he said. "I ain't a lifeguard."

"You said that already," I told him.

"That jerk social worker shouldn't have let them put those canoes in. You can't canoe in waves that high, not in Lake Michigan. What kind of stupidity is that anyway? – geez."

"He didn't know."

"He should've."

"You talk to him at all?"

"I sold him the sticker is all. Don't even remember him. Long hair, I think. A beard. He said the guys kept their rooms clean. 'Which way is the beach?' he says. 'These guys got a day off for keeping their rooms clean.' He says it for them, looking around toward the back seat, you know—not for me."

"That's all you remember?"

"Shoot, and I'm going, 'I don't even keep my room clean.'"

"So he didn't know anything?" I said.

"Guy with half a brain could see you can't canoe when the water's up. That don't take any smarts."

"So it's his fault?" I said.

"Guy like that doesn't know the lake. They shouldn't send anybody down here who doesn't know the lake."

"Who's they?" I said.

"The guy's boss. I don't know. Whoever sent him down to the park. How am I supposed to know? It's just not my fault."

He sat with his elbows on his legs, toying with a ski rope, his broad shoulders—like his mother's family—squared, his thick arms packed into the jacket. At fourteen he stopped wearing my shirts because his chest didn't get into them anymore, but big as he is, he's not strong enough to carry those dead boys.

"You been looking for that body, haven't you?" I told him. "You were out last night and you're out again tonight because you want to find it."

"Can't a guy take a walk on the lake?" he said.

"No law against it," I told him. It was early. It couldn't have been much past eight. I figured I could help him somehow, maybe I had to. "Do the lights work on the Farmall?" I said. "You used it when you were seining smelt, didn't you?"

"They work," he said.

"Maybe we ought to take a ride," I told him.

He turned around on his seat, looked right at me.

"You never know," I said.

He shook his head. "I looked half the morning. Cecil put me on the tractor and sent me up and down the beach, one end of the park to the other. He says we just as soon not have people bumping into that thing by surprise."

"You had enough?" I asked.

He looked down at his watch. "It's Saturday night," I told him. "You haven't been home this early in years."

*

I let him drive. I sat up on the fender, and the lights gave us enough illumination for us to spot a body up on shore or still rolling in shallow water. The air was cool and damp, of course, so I grabbed a couple stocking caps while Brad was getting the tractor out of the shed. I pulled on another sweater and told Ann what we were up to. She'd been reading.

"What are you going to do if you find it?" she said, taking off her glasses.

"I don't think we will," I told her, grabbing Brad's heavy jacket.

"Then why are you looking?"

"I'm going along for the ride," I told her. "He's the one that's looking."

We rode on the slant of the beach edge, six miles down to the mouth of the river, as far as we could go. Some places where the beach is gone, he'd slow down and take the water, the lights bouncing off the surface in a way that made me afraid we'd feel some clunk, then turn and watch a face or an arm or a leg emerge from the track of the big wheel beneath me.

When we got to the Sauk, he stood at the edge of the river, the lights disappearing into the water and the wispy fog. He pushed the gas back to an idle, and stared for a moment, and I knew he was thinking about the river currents out into the lake, about what they might do to that last body, how they might fan its drift miles down the beach, far beyond us, south even to Chicago. I know he was thinking that. I know it.

"That's it," I told him, over the engine noise.

He reached for the gearshift between his legs and swiveled around to back up over the dry sand, and he never said a thing. We went faster back up the beach towards home, our tracks, where they were visible, like a reminder that we'd covered all this ground already and no real goal could be found anyway. I didn't think the Lord would wash him up like that—just for us.

He pulled off the hat I'd given him and stuck it in his pocket, then stood up, keeping both hands on the wheel, his eyes moving back and forth over the beach—going too fast, I thought.

When I used to fish out there with Brad, Ann said she could hear us talk no matter how far out we went, our voices carrying through the open stillness as if there could be no secrets on the lake. That night I wondered what the people thought up and down the beach when they heard us go by, not once but twice, and saw a huddled figure in a stocking cap leaning on the fender of a tractor driven by a boy standing up and staring at the water as if he might find some monumental treasure tossed up by the wash of an evening's gentle waves.

We never spoke during that long ride. But I knew that if I tried to yell over the engine's heavy popping, I'd be heard by the whole world. Every word. So I kept quiet because it seemed to me then that I had something to say that wasn't meant for a crowd.

Brad needed that body, needed to pull it himself from the maw of the killer lake, as if he were in fact the lifeguard he swore he never was, as if he still could rescue someone already dead for two days. But it wasn't that boy he needed to rescue. I think it was himself.

*

Sunday morning came as perfect as a storybook Easter. Ann stayed in bed and I brought her coffee, along with the front page of the Journal. I read all of the sports before Jeremy got up to grab the funnies and Sarah came down asking about Brad.

"He isn't in his room?" I said.

Ann must have heard Sarah's announcement.

"Maybe he stayed overnight someplace," Sarah said. Ann came up behind her and shrugged her shoulders.

When I went out back to the boat shed, I saw the Farmall was gone and I wondered how on earth he could start that thing without either of us hearing it. I saw the tracks through the pine needles out back, and watched the gouges run west down the lake road instead of east past the side of the house. He didn't want me along. I walked out to the water and looked both ways along the shore. A single track ran north up the beach towards the park. A man in a brown hunting coat walked his collie my way, maybe fifty yards up, just past Vandiver's, so I waited.

"You didn't see a tractor, did you," I said, "Farmall, an old orange one?"

"Nobody out here but me and Pepper," he said.

A blue-green choppy mask broke into rippling waves just off shore, little waves, as if the hand of God were somewhere just beneath the whole lake rocking it gently.

"He's still looking?" Ann said when I got back to the house.

"Where is he?" Sarah said. "Is he fishing or what?"

In a way, I guess, he was.

*

Church starts at ten, and he goes with us every Sunday whether or not he wants to. It's a rule we have. As long as he lives with us, he lives by our rules—and our rules include church. I'm a believer, always have been. Not that I don't have doubts, but so did King David sometimes.

We were all dressed up and ready by the time I heard the Farmall roll up the beach. I didn't say a thing when he came in the front door and left the tractor stand out front.

His face—his eyes—seemed vacant, and there was a hollowness in his voice. "I found it," he said. "It was only about a mile up from the park. Can you believe that?"

Ann looked at me from across the table as if he'd just said something really profane.

"You leave it there?" I said. It was a stupid question, but I didn't know what to say.

"I called from a cottage. It's already picked up—"

"What'd you find?" Sarah said out of nowhere.

I waited for him to answer that question because I wanted to know what he'd say. But he looked at me as if I were the only one with the voice.

"He found the body of the boy who drowned Friday," I told her, gently pushing the designer's tag down into the back of the neck of her summer dress.

"Wow," she said, and she pulled a hand up to her face.

It was Jeremy who said it, even though I wondered myself at that very moment, and I'm sure Ann did too.

"What'd it look like?" he said.

I've seen Brad speechless for the last four years, but I never saw him so robbed of words. He ripped open the clasps of his jacket and stripped it off his shoulders, all the while looking down at the want ads on the table.

"Was it all blue or what?" Jeremy said.

He's ten, and he's seen his share of TV death.

"Sometimes sand rubs off all the hair," Jeremy said to all of us, as if we really wanted to know.

I kept waiting for Brad. He threw the coat over the love seat and looked right into his little brother's eyes. "He was dead," he said. "Nothing spectacular or nothing. He was just plain dead."

And then he looked at me, as if I had a sermon.

*

We've never had a day's worry with our Mary. This summer she's working in a student ministry in Sequoia National Park. During the week, she scoops ice cream in a fancy concession in a tourist trap, and on Sundays she helps out in a little park ministry that meets in the forest, logs for pews.

But Brad has always been another story. Mary professed her faith and took communion when she was fourteen, stood up in front of the church all alone and answered the questions. I remember how the preacher gave her this little hug up front once it was over, and neither Ann nor I will ever forget her smile.

Brad is already four years older than Mary was when she told the whole church that she loved Jesus. Some Sunday mornings we almost have to dress him to get him there. I'd rather not know, sometimes, how he spends his Saturday nights. When he goes to college next year, I'm sure Ann and I will spend more time praying for that boy than we have for Mary in all of her years.

Brad's never said a thing about faith to me, not one thing. We haven't forced him. He's never professed his faith. I don't think he's any kind of agnostic; he just lets it go somehow because it's part of the baggage of his parents' values—it's what he's rebelling from, I suppose, part of the world he thinks he has to leave in order to become who he will be.

I've asked the Lord to make this sullenness of his, this rebellion, this dark kind of brooding, strengthen him someday, so that in some future time his sneering, like Paul's, would make him a saint. But I haven't seen a thing yet to assure me I've been heard.

We had communion this morning. Sometimes I wish I were a Catholic so that I could say that this bread and wine is more than just a symbol, more than just grape juice and a dry cube of bread that points at a higher reality. In our church, that's all it is—a token remembrance of Christ's shed blood and broken body. You eat it and drink it to prompt a memory some don't have. At times, I wish it were the real flesh and blood.

So I'm sitting there this morning waiting for the bread and the wine, Brad right there beside me, chewing his fingernails, his knee up against the pew in front of us. But I knew it was different for him this time, because I knew that the blue face of a boy drowned for almost three days hung in his mind, a face he claimed he really hadn't seen that Friday morning in the back of the van, a face he'd seen for the first startling time that very Sunday dawn.

When the sun rises over the lake, it gilds everything with a sheen that's heavenly gold. But I knew that morning that nothing the sun could do could wipe away death from the face of a boy who could have known that taking out a canoe in surf swept up by a rough east wind was dangerous—if only he'd known, if someone who knew had told him as much. No gold lay over that face in the lakeshore dawn.

So I grabbed Brad's hand once the bread had been passed. I grabbed it and I opened those fingers stained with state park green paint. I opened it to calluses and a width that long ago surpassed my pink banker's hands, and I shoved that bread there in his palm, even though he's not supposed to partake, not having professed. I force-fed my son the body of Christ.

"Take eat, remember and believe," the preacher said, and an entire church—all except me— raised the body to lips waiting for the relief of our own guilt, sin washed forever out to sea in the blood of Christ's death.

And Brad looked at me as a child might have, as he might have himself before he'd become the problem we'd prayed about for so long. With my thumb I pointed at my mouth.

His eyes glazed almost, not in tears but in fear.

"Take it," I said. "Go on—you know what it is."

And I grabbed his hand again and raised it, held it up to his face until he took the bread into his mouth, held it there until it turned, as the Catholic in me prayed it would—just today—into the body I know he needed so badly to find.

"Remember and believe that the body of our Lord was broken for all our sins," the preacher said.

And I pulled his hand back down from his lips and held it the way I used to, the way, years ago, he once wanted me to.

And I'm the one who cried.

Exodus

Even though it came first, Nebraska seemed the longest stretch, land so flat and ordinary, so dark green in August along the Platte, but only the start of a long trip he and Eleanor had taken what?–ten times and even more. Coming up on the silhouette of the Rockies was always a thrill otherwise, the mountains in an outline of haze, Pike's Peak on the right when finally you turn south to New Mexico. That pretty red rock he'd missed in the darkness, driving all night, the dawn finally coming up in his rearview when he'd turned west again from Albuquerque. Then, desert country so naked he felt forever guilty about what the white man had done in giving it up like some prize to the Indians. A whole day and a whole night he'd spent on the road before that three-hour drop-off from Flagstaff to Phoenix, a road where you spend more time footing the brake than the gas. A long, long ways he'd driven, even though it didn't seem that far now that he was there, and he never once got tired because the Lord knows this was no pleasure trip and he didn't spend a moment sight-seeing. It was a good thing he'd bought that Travelall for the boat because he needed the space to move Janna's stuff back—and the kids.

Wilfred Staab had his own reasons why his daughter's marriage had failed, and it had less to do with Craig's drinking than it did with what his son-in-law did for a living—police work. Television said it all the time, how cops couldn't come home without dragging the job along; but it wasn't just that either, he thought, since nobody worth his salt can go home and turn it off just like that, whether it was laying concrete or raising hogs or catching crooks. It wasn't just being good at what you did; it was what Craig did specifically—being a cop and always having to see so much evil. That's what did him in, Wilf thought. That's what made him drink, and that's what did in their whole dream of living in Arizona—Craig and Janna, who'd hardly ever been out of Iowa, and their two little ones, who, since their parents had moved to the Promised Land, had hardly ever been back home.

He parked the truck in front of a 7-11 across the road from the station where he stopped to refuel, then went inside and asked for quarters, five bucks worth, even though he didn't mean to make a long call, just to tell Eleanor he'd arrived. Almost 26 hours, straight through, but he wouldn't have to tell her how long because Eleanor would know the minute the phone rang.

The instructions were in two languages, one of them Spanish, but the place was full of Mexicans, jabbering just like Vietnamese used to back in Saigon, as if they were all hard of hearing. He knew what kind of target he made too—this old overweight white guy driving a Travelall with Iowa plates—easy tourist pickins, and he'd heard far too many of Craig's horror stories, so many in fact that if Craig were his own boy, he'd have told him to cool it with the blood and guts. Back home, Craig could get a crowd in church or at the bowling alley or anywhere downtown inside five minutes, everybody wanting to hear what life was like for a big-city cop—all the gory details, how people are pigs.

Scared?—yeah, darn right scared, he told himself, just like Vietnam. I'm a fish out of water here, and he'd have likely told the operator exactly that if those three hombres standing by the air hose had come any closer while he had the phone in his hand. Scared?—sure as shit, scared, he told himself, but mad too, and full of hate and not for them either.

Even the operator was Mexican. She told him that he couldn't use quarters on this pay phone, that if he'd like to call long distance he had to use his card. "I don't have a card," he told her. Or else reverse charges. "Then reverse charges," he said, "make it collect," and immediately he felt dumb for not thinking of it himself. So now what was he going to do with a pocket full of quarters jingling in his pants like a come-on?

"Your name, sir?" she said. Behind her voice, the phone back home was already ringing. He glanced at his watch, then remembered Iowa was an hour later.

"Wilf Staab," he said, "S-T-A-A-B. But she'll know my name—it's my wife I'm calling."

The phone line bleated three times before Eleanor picked it up.

"I'm here," he told her after the operator let them alone. "You know where we always get gas? I'm across the street." One of the kids whipped an empty bottle into the air. It turned and gleamed in the bright lights and crashed in a dark parking lot next door. "She call?"

"Four, five hours ago or so. Wondered when you'd get there," Eleanor told him. "She's not crying. Seemed to me the kids were quiet—at least I didn't hear 'em."

"You okay?" he said.

"Worked my fingers to the bone on that couch of Eric and AnnLynn," she said. "You should'a' let me come along, you know."

"A whole day in that truck with you, and I'd be dead," he said. "You just make the nest. Keep yourself busy 'till you can't anymore, and then hit the sack. You can figure when we'll be back."

"What time is it?" she said.

"Hour earlier than it is up there," he told her.

"I'm not thinking well," she told him.

"Was *he* there?"

"What do you mean?"

"Was Craig there when Janna called?"

"No, but I don't remember, Wilf. I'm all upset. Now you be careful–you hear me? You keep a civil tongue and all, and–"

"You know me. I can't talk. I'm just like Moses," he told her.

"Just bring her home, sweetheart," she said. "Make sure they got toys out when you leave so the kids got something to play with in the truck."

"Whyn't you make something out of those blueberries you bought?" he said. "Cobbler or something, something the kids'll like?"

"I got a ton of muffin mix all ready, and I canned some–"

"Just try to get some sleep then," he said. "Everything's going to be fine. I'm going to bring your daughter home."

"It isn't fine, Wilf, and you know it," she told him.

"Well then at least it's going to be better tomorrow than it was today. Think of it that way."

When he put down the phone, the first thing he heard was the whine of a siren, and he thought the same thing he always did when they visited their kids–how some people get used to that sound when they hear it all the time. He picked up the quarters, and turned back to his truck in thick desert heat that always seemed to him unnatural.

The boys he'd seen at the side of the building were coming his way—three of them, all of them taller than he was. He stood up straight like military. He hadn't dressed up for this trip. He'd gone home right away, as soon as Eleanor had come to where they were pouring concrete to tell him Janna said to come pick her up because she couldn't take it anymore. He'd filled up with gas, picked up some cash, and left town in a half hour—never even changed clothes, streaks of concrete still on his jeans. Right then he was happy about that. He'd have felt scared in Sunday clothes or a sport shirt. Work clothes were like fatigues.

"Mister," one of the boys said, "you got any cash?"

He'd already had his hands in his pockets, so he scooped out the quarters, all twenty of them, and rolled them in his hands until he had them in a stack, then grabbed the hand of the kid who'd asked and banged them in his palm. "Now get lost," he said, "before I whale on your ass."

Scared?—sure, he thought, as he got back into the truck he bought just for fishing, but maybe he shouldn't have said what he did exactly.

*

He came back on the freeway from Grant Road, and wondered who could have ever guessed that after eleven years without kids, in a matter of days they'd have two back in town. Already a year after he'd started medical school, their son Eric had been courted by local doctors who wanted him to consider family practice in Neukirk. He and Eleanor hadn't tried to push him to come back—push *them*—because AnnLynn was a part of the decision, what she wanted. They wanted their kids back in town, but they wanted what was best for them first and foremost; and if Eric and AnnLynn felt some other town was a better option, then that was just fine too. Eleanor came home with the news even before Eric had called to tell them. She knew he'd signed because Doc Beckering told her. They acted surprised anyway, when Eric called. Played the fool.

And now Janna. Not that they didn't know things were bad. Janna was always stubborn and hard, not one to complain but never one to throw in the towel. He pulled back into the traffic and remembered the night he and Eleanor had figured this boy—and Janna'd had her choices all right—that this Craig was going to be something special. They had lay in bed talking that night about how you couldn't choose your kids' mates, how really powerless parents were in such a big decision.

"You don't like this guy?" he asked her, looking up at the little glowing stars Eleanor had pasted up on their bedroom ceiling years before.

"It's not that," she said. "It doesn't just come out of nowhere is what I'm saying. I can see why she loves him."

"What's he do?" he'd said.

"It's not so much what he does as who he is—"

"Okay, then what is he?" he'd asked.

She waited a minute. "He's a whole lot like her father," she said, laughing.

A long time ago already, when Janna didn't call and didn't write, and when finally both of them could tell she was faking the good times, when she seemed more blessed cheery about things than she'd ever once been, they figured it all for the worst. They weren't foolish, and they'd understood that at least part of the reason for leaving Iowa was this sense that maybe they needed a new start some hope.

"He drinks too much," she told them a year ago. "Way too much, and I get mad too often," she said, her voice letting out words like steam. Wherever she'd leave gaps, Wilf filled them in with the worst—just as Eleanor must have on the kitchen phone. He had trouble trying to know who to feel for most—Eleanor, who was upstairs bundling Kleenex, or his only daughter, who probably had it a worse than she was letting on, if he knew her.

"Maybe you ought to try AA or something," he said, because he knew Eleanor wasn't about to try to talk just then. "You talk to your pastor ever?"

Silence. "You know me," Janna says.

Nobody said a word.

"What am I supposed to do?" she'd said.

He's got the two women closest to him in all the world on separate ends of the phone he's got in his hands, both of them full of hurt, and the two of them leave it up to him to say the right thing, a man who can lay a three-car driveway in half a morning without a ripple but isn't worth a quarter at picking words out of the fray.

"You see if you can't work it out," he told her. "We're not asking for a miracle here, and if things don't get any better, you call. But he's your husband, and you swore to it." That's what he told her—something like that, only maybe not as pretty.

For a year, they'd never heard a word. Vacation came and went—the whole family back to Iowa. Nothing. No mention. Craig out with his old buddies, the three of them home alone at night, kids in bed, and still nothing. Janna could have spilled her guts right there in the family room where she'd grown up watching cartoons, and not a comment. So the moment she left, Eleanor cried.

"Just like my wife to think the sky's falling," he told her. They were standing at the door, the minivan barely out of the driveway. He had to take her in his arms.

"Never once the whole time did they even touch," she told him. "You see that, Wilf?" she said. "Never once."

"So?" he said. "They got two kids and they been married long enough. All that goosy shit is over."

She dug her face into his shoulder.

*

The boy, Kurtis, was awfully young for glasses, Wilf thought, but cuter than a bug's ear anyway. So studious-like, he looked like his uncle Eric, the big-shot doctor. He sat on the couch with a book that looked way too heavy for a boy his age, never really said much when his grandpa showed up, just smiled. Right then, Wilf felt bad that he'd not changed; if he'd looked presentable the kids would have maybe taken a shine to him—although they hadn't seen their grandparents all that often, twice a year only since they'd been born.

Gracie was reading too, and it made him wonder about how all of this was affecting the kids, whether maybe they were hiding between the covers. She was a doll, toothless, that perfectly blonde hair falling light as down to her shoulders.

Janna was heavier again, not that he wanted to blame her. Everybody's got to take refuge somewhere. She was wearing a sleeveless blouse, the kind her mother wore around the house in the summer, and shorts that were too much a reminder of what she used to weigh. He hugged her, but it was awkward because it always was with Janna. Even when she was a baby, she didn't take to being held. Janna was a cat, Eric a dog. Janna had a mind of her own. Eric always tried to please—Eagle Scout, track star, what not. Janna wasn't a bad kid, but she'd never really given the sense that she needed her parents at all, not really. She had her share of hard times—seemed, sometimes, to choose them.

The first thing she did when he came in—after the hug and seeing the kids, was stick a cup of coffee in his hand and take him out through the dining room door and into the garage, where she already had the goods lined up—four suitcases, a Ninja Turtles duffle bag, two thick garment bags, and a pair of backpacks loaded with goodies for the trip.

"Where's *he*?" Wilf asked when they walked back into the dining room.

"Working."

"He knows?"

Janna ran a twist of hair back behind her ears and bit her lip. "He knows," she said, "you can bet he even knows you're here. He's got his buddies watching out for him."

"Cops?" Wilf asked.

Hate was in her eyes. "They watch me constantly—they do."

Behind her, up on the wall at the door to the garage was a bulletin board full of kids' finger paintings, a list of numbers, and that ugly church picture of Grandpa and Grandma Staab Eleanor had sent.

"Don't tell me to stay, Dad," she told him.

"I didn't come all the way down here for nothing," he said. "I could'a told you that over the phone for a buck-and-a-half."

She smiled.

"So what's the plan?" he said.

"You must be tired," she told him. "You must be shot."

"Not as young as I used to be," he told her. "It's too hot to lay cement anyway."

"I thought you quit for your shoulders' sake," she said. "I thought you sold the business."

"I did," he told her. "But Buddy's so busy that he can't do without me. That's how valuable I am, even with my shoulders shot."

"I thought you were going to do nothing but fish," she said.

"Just dreams."

She shook her head like she knew about dreams. These little bits of the real her you had to pick up on–a smile once in a while, a tip of her head, a twitch in her eyes. That was her language, always was. She didn't give a thing away.

"I'm sorry about all this," he said. "Your mother and I–" He didn't know exactly how to put it. He looked up at that bulletin board. How in heck could he tell her how dead her mother felt about it, how she'd told him one night that she didn't think she could ever make love again, not with her daughter in the kind of big trouble Eleanor thought she was?

"It just didn't work, Dad," she told him.

"From the start?"

She shrugged her shoulders. "Maybe I shouldn't have married him. It was the big thing back home, you know–getting out the house and getting married."

Up on that bulletin board she'd hung a picture of the Colorado Rockies with a little inscription–"Ain't no mountain high enough" and some Bible verse printed in such little print he couldn't read it without glasses. Had to be a Colorado mountain, Wilf figured, because no Arizona mountain was that kind of snowy beautiful.

"I can't anymore. I tried," she told him. "I just can't."

"I know you did, Janna," he told her. "You're our daughter."

"Mom told me once how mad she used to get mad at you. She told me about a time you had some kind of family picnic or something, and all day long, she said, how you played volleyball with all the men, while she had to run after kids and get this and get that, and put all the food out and whatnot, and how it wore her out, Dad."

Could have been a hundred picnics, he thought.

"She said you were coming home that night in all that heat–"

"In Iowa?" he said.

"Yes, in Iowa. It's worse in Iowa, Dad, believe me." That was the old Janna. "You were coming home on the blacktop from Neukirk. Mom says she can remember the exact spot. She says she'll never forget it. She says you turned to her and you said, 'Boy, that was fun. That was a great day.' And she says she was so mad she says she could have got out of the car and walked home. She says she'll never forget the exact spot on that blacktop, Dad, the exact spot where you said that."

"I did that?" he said.

"She says you never thought about her that day, chasing kids and keeping them happy. And I asked her how she could do it and you know what she said, Dad?"

He shook his head.

"'You just gotta' love him. I love your father'–that's what she told me." She looked him straight in the eye. "I don't love Craig," she said. "Not anymore anyway."

He couldn't get the garage door open because for a minute he couldn't figure out the lock. Dang shame anyway, he thought, people having to lock up garages. What kind of life you got when you can't trust the neighbors?

Once he got it open, he backed the truck up the driveway like a moving van, and inside a couple of minutes he had the kids' seats strapped in and everything loaded–whatever Janna had packed and plenty of room to spare.

"How come you took the bikes, Grandpa?" Kurtis said, flicking his glasses up on his nose. "Your Grandma and I gonna' want to try these things out," he told him. "These are beauties—"

"They're not for big people," the boy said, scolding him. "They're for kids."

He stopped dead in his tracks. "You aren't kidding?" he said. "Maybe we ought to let 'em here then."

Kurtis pursed his lips. "Can I ride at your house?" he asked.

"All day long if you like—all over town too," he said. "Tell you what—why don't we keep 'em in the truck in case you want to tool around?"

"Okay with me," the boy said.

He picked up Kurtis and hiked him up on his arm. "Grandma says she's got blueberry muffins just growing in the kitchen. She says you shouldn't be eating anything all the way back to Iowa, just saving up room for those muffins."

"I love muffins," Kurtis said.

"Grandmas know that. They got lists of what kids like," he told him.

The boy pointed over his shoulder. "It's daddy," he said, and he scrambled to get down.

The tall blonde guy getting out of the squad car didn't look like the Craig he wanted to see. He remembered what Eleanor had said the first time she saw him after he got the job: "there's something about a uniform." And what was worse was the way

Kurtis ran down the driveway just to get to his father, so much like he loved him.

Right then he'd have given anything for a trowel and a pail of mush. Rather than face the talking he was going to have to do, he'd have traded places with any mason in the whole valley, even though it was hot as hades. Like Jonah, or Moses, he thought. He got those two stuck in his craw because the both of them complained to the Lord they couldn't get the words out.

Craig was down at the end of the driveway, sort of nuzzling his son's hair and looking for all the world like the father Wilf figured he wasn't. "So much like you," Eleanor had told him—and not just that first night either, but later, at the wedding, at the reception when Craig and Janna walked from table to table greeting the families and well-wishers, Craig standing there straight as a beam, looking like for a dime he'd rather be out somewhere filling silo, while Janna—who really wasn't all that much better at being sweetheartish—led him around like a mule. "You were the same way," Eleanor told him that night at the head table. "I was so mad at you."

He'd pointed at Craig. "It's all he cares about is the honeymoon," he said. "I can't blame him."

It was blue, the uniform, full of badges and what not, his waist thick as a roofer's with tools of the trade, the gun leaning away from his hip on the right side, things hanging all over. But neat. His hair was cut shorter than Wilf remembered, even styled, and he didn't look at all like a drunk.

"Kurtis, you run inside now," Craig told his son. "Go see what Mom's up to."

Wilf wiped his hands on his pants and walked out the open garage to meet him. Scared? Sure, he thought. Give me the words, Lord.

"I been thinking," Craig said when he came up. "You're my father too, you know? Not just hers anymore."

Wilf lifted his cap and wiped back the sweat. "That's true in the books," he said.

Craig raised his eyebrows enough to let him know he didn't like it. "You don't know the half of it," he said. "You don't know anything but what your daughter tells you."

Down there around his belt there was belly hanging already, and he wasn't even 35, Wilf thought. Without the uniform, he wouldn't have been such a big shot, doughy in the face, red in the cheeks like an alcoholic, a man who looked like he could have had a heart attack long before his time.

"You don't want to hear the other side?" Craig said.

"I'll listen," Wilf said, "but right now I'm bringing my daughter home."

Something came up in Craig's throat. "We can lick this," he said, choking something back, "but I can't do it without her."

Wilf shook his head. "Well, you're going to have to, because I didn't drive all this way for nothing."

"I won't let you," he said, his eyes jumping from the brickwork to the garage and the bushes, the landscaping. "I'm not letting you take my family."

"You aren't the law this time," he said, "even if you're wearing a uniform."

"Then who is?" he snarled.

Wilf looked at the truck. "I guess it's me."

"On whose authority?"

"My own." He thumbed at his chest.

The kid was ripped up. You could see it. "I'm in counseling now, all right?" he said. "Dang it, Wilf, I'm doing what I'm supposed to be doing."

"Aren't you on duty?"

"Yes."

"Then clean up these streets, all right? Get out of the way," Wilf told him. "I'll be glad to talk about this once we get back home. I'll talk forever. But right now I'm getting her out of here, and there ain't nothing more to say."

"Don't do this, Dad, all right? Stay over tonight. Stay in our house here and we can talk. We can start over. We can sit down over coffee and you can hear me out for once. You must be tired—"

"I got a full tank of what I been running on."

"Don't do this to me, Wilf," he said. "Don't do this."

"It's nothing I'm doing to you, Craig," he said. "What I'm doing, I'm doing for her. What comes after this is what the two of you got to do together." He rubbed the sweat from the corner of his lips with the back of his wrist. "Don't fight it now because it's a done thing."

That whole time Janna was loading the kids behind them, strapping them in the back seat, checking through the stuff Wilf had loaded in the back of the truck. She threw in her purse and whatever other goodies she'd tucked along. Craig stood there in his uniform, his hands tucked in his back pockets, looking almost like a baby, Wilf thought, sadder than anything. Maybe there was hope.

"Where's Daddy going to sit, Mom?" Kurtis said, once she had him in good.

That question hung in the silence like the sound of a siren.

"Mommy's got plenty of books," she said, showing the kids the big shopping bag up in the front seat. She climbed in the front seat.

"Daddy?" Kurtis said.

"You got a map?" Janna asked.

"I know the way," Wilf told her.

"You got gas? I got money," she said.

"It's already filled," he said.

"C'mon Daddy," Gracie said.

Somebody had to say something, he thought. "Your daddy's coming later," Wilf said. "He's got to work, and then he's coming by himself."

Janna pulled the shoulder harness around her and locked it in place. Kurtis reached out with both hands for a kiss from his father, and Craig obliged, crawling into the back seat to give both a hug. Wilf stood outside the driver's side, Janna acting like her husband was some kind of desert snake, then he went back to the garage and pulled down the door.

Through the back of the van, through the handlebars of the bikes, he saw Craig hold on to every last minute, and he was struck with the sense that the kids, both of them, looked more like their father than they did like Janna. Craig pulled himself back a bit from Gracie, touched his lip with his pointer and tapped the tip of her nose.

Janna turned and ripped out the seat belt, then stepped back out of the truck. "Get him out of here, Dad," she said. "Let's go. Get him out of here."

He stood at the back of the truck, as both of the kids wouldn't let their father go. "Good Lord," he said to himself, "give me a map out of this." Maybe he ought to stay, he thought. Maybe he ought to just sit here with the two of them until things settled down or something. Maybe hauling them off wasn't the right thing to do. Twenty minutes ago he'd been sure that the only question was going to be how long all of this was going to take, how much time to pack the car and have them aimed back towards the Midwest.

Craig slowly untangled himself from his kids and backed out of the seat, stood there with the door open, looking at him. "Look at what you're doing to them," he said, just like that, talking way too loud. "Look once what you're doing to my kids," and then he pointed at them, as if they weren't kids at all, nothing with blood and a heart.

He shouldn't have said something like that in front of the kids, Wilf thought. He walked around the passenger's side, stepped between his son-in-law and the door, and shut it softly. "Now get back in that car or go in the house or do whatever you're supposed to do," he told Craig, "or else I'm going to call a real cop."

Just like that he was all words. Craig blew out a whole lot of things in a tone of voice he shouldn't have used, words that could have been forgiven, Wilf thought, if it hadn't have been for the kids right there beside him, their doors and windows closed, but his own door still open like a gash. It wasn't the words so much as the pitch of his voice that the kids wouldn't forget, the sound of an animal wounded, their father.

Big as owls their eyes were when he got into the truck. He started the engine as quickly as he could and pulled it into gear, but Craig ran out front and stood directly in the way, the look on his face rock-solid. Janna said, "that son of a bitch," and Wilf reached across the seat and grabbed her wrist. "Don't let me ever hear you say that about their father again," he said.

"Well, look at him," she said, eyes like notched spears.

He wanted to cry, not for himself but for all of them and the damned darkness all around that try as you might you never could quite turn your back on–hate, pure and simple evil he could feel even in the way he was, right then, pinching his daughter's arm.

"You're not going," Craig screamed and he put both hands up against hood as if by force of will he could stop them.

The kids didn't have to hear another word, he thought as he got out of the truck again and shut his door behind him, keeping hold of the handle. "I'll run you down, Craig, I swear it," he said as quietly as he could. "You better believe me when I say I'm right now bringing Janna home."

"You'll kill me for what *she* says?" He pointed at the front seat. At least he didn't scream. "You don't even know the whole story, and you'll run me down?"

"I ain't going to hurt nobody here if you get out of the way," Wilf told him, slowly, quietly. "What I'm saying is, soon as I get back to Iowa I'll call you and we can talk forever. But right now, I got to leave–*we* got to leave."

"Then leave my kids behind," he said.

"Who's going to care for them, Craig?" he said. "Who's got the time with you off to work? Don't be stupid." He pointed at the squad car. "Get back to work. Once things cool off here–tell you what, I'll pay for a ticket. You fly home."

Craig took his hands off the hood but stayed in front of the truck, backed off just enough for Wilf to think it was his turn to act, so he threw open the door and jumped in without looking at his son-in-law, as if trusting him to give it up. But when he got back behind the wheel, Craig still held his ground.

Janna should never have done it, but she did. She rolled down her window and screamed at him. She said, "Get out of the way." That's all, nothing else at first, but it wasn't so much what she said either as the way she laced those words with hate. "You son-of-a-bitch," she screamed at him, "get out of the way." Right in front of the kids.

Whatever it was that set him off so fast he didn't even change clothes back in Neukirk, whatever force pushed him to drive down here as if going to Arizona was a trip to Sioux Falls, whatever fire was in his belly all the way down went out maybe because Janna didn't seem so much his daughter, someone who needed him, as someone who needed something a whole lot more than anything a father could ever begin to think about providing.

He reached over, but at that moment, she yelled, "Go ahead," and he looked back up at Craig, who had that service revolver out and pointed right at Janna, his elbows down on the hood, the gun in both hands like you see on TV. "Go ahead," she yelled again. "You don't have the guts," she said.

And just like that, Craig stood up from the aim he'd taken, stood straight and tall and turned that gun on himself, swung it up towards his mouth, and in that flash, that half-second Wilf finally did exactly what he'd threatened, without even thinking. Even before Craig got that barrel in his mouth, Wilf hit the gas and the truck lunged forward like some tethered beast and knocked him down. There was no sudden clunk because Craig wasn't so much smacked by the force as he was shoved hard to the cement.

"You stay in the truck," he yelled at his daughter, and in those few seconds—three maybe—that it took for him to get around the hood to the front, he thought of so many possibilities that it seemed almost as if he might be the one about to die. Concussion—and he saw Craig in a hospital bed like some swami, head in bandages. Pinned beneath the truck—he'd have to call on the Lord for the great strength, like farm women lifting tractors miraculously off their husbands. And even as his mind was riffling through scenes, he waited for a shot from that pistol that would have ended it in the way Craig had threatened.

What he saw before anything else was the pistol, maybe three feet from Craig's right hand, and the first thing he did was stick it in his pants. Craig was up on one elbow, his face seemed turned at an angle, like a dog that hears something strange in the wind, woozy as if he'd hit his head. "You're my son all right," he told him, "and I'm not going to forget it." He picked him up by the shoulders and dragged him across the driveway and laid him in the grass. Then he got back in the truck, slammed the door, and the Travelall bumped softly down the end of the driveway as he turned it right, toward 35th Avenue.

"He okay?" Janna said.

He didn't dare look back at the kids, but he knew he couldn't let Craig lie there in the grass, helpless. He reached for the sweatshirt he kept beneath the seat, stopped the truck when he was alongside the police car, jumped out once more. "I'll call you, I swear," he said as he laid the sweatshirt over his son-in-law's shoulders. "We got to make something out of this," he said. "It can't end this way."

Craig pulled himself up and held his head with both hands. Wilf got to his feet and went to the car. If he could operate the radio, he'd call something in, he thought, so he opened the door and picked up the handset, tried clicking it, making it squawk, but there was nothing. He looked up and down the dash for some kind of switch for the lights, and he when he found it, he snapped it on so red and orange flashes danced across the panel on top, sending colored lights banging off the front of the houses up and down the street.

He wasn't thinking so much about the kids when he got back inside because Janna was crying now, and for that he was thankful. He came up to the traffic on 35th and pulled into the right lane, going south toward Thunderbird. If he'd taken his work truck, he could have used the CB, but he figured the lights would pull in a crowd and somebody would see Craig there on the street, somebody would help him. Hadn't Janna said that his cop buddies were always looking out for him? It was all he could do now to get some distance on the whole mess, separate them for a while, cool the whole business down, bring some silence.

He saw Janna sneak a peek at her kids as they came to the freeway entrance, and he turned right into the cloverleaf and took that long curve so slow it seemed they weren't leaving all that trouble behind in the dust and the darkness of the desert. A pair of courteous eighteen-wheelers swept into the left lane to give him room, and he was on his way home.

The lights of the north suburbs gradually tailed off with each mile they passed in the silence outside the big city. He didn't have a thing to say to her. If there were some way he could draw a partition up between them, like a taxi, he'd have done it because he didn't have a good thing to say to his daughter right then, nothing sweet. It wasn't at all like he imagined it, he thought, wasn't at all like Moses taking people out of trouble, wasn't that way at all, he thought, not the kind of joy he thought he'd feel doing the right thing.

Ten miles north of 35th and Thunderbird, the lights from the city finally stayed behind them, the tail-end of a long clear desert day still glowing over the ridge of mountains west, a ridge cut jagged by the purple dusk. The only thing lit in front of them now were green Interstate signs and here and there a billboard. He looked over the gauges in front of him. Tank was full. The truck rolled heavily, the engine pulling a bit, the gas pedal low to the floor beneath his boot, even though they weren't speeding and not about to, not with Craig's friends in uniform. They were going uphill, he remembered. All the way to Flagstaff it was a climb.

Perfect silence in the truck. Just so there'd be something, he turned on the radio and something country and western came up with so much volume he turned it down so there wasn't much more than a beat and faintest hint of melody. The faint reach of the interior lights weren't enough for him to see anything of the kids in the rearview mirror, little more than a shine off Kurtis's glasses.

So he tried to run away for just a minute. He looked out to what was left of a sunny day. Somewhere out there west, he thought, if you go far enough into that ridge of mountains that wouldn't disappear, if you climbed high enough to get out of the desert cactus and those thick bushes that crawled all over the hills, up high enough somewhere you'd find pines probably, and somewhere a lake, perfectly blue, like the sky above it, and about a thousand trout or walleye or pike or whatever, a little lake so still it'd be a shame to start a motor. You could take a canoe out there, pack some bait in, and a couple of rods, and spend a day talking to nobody whatsoever, nobody but worms and some fish and the Good Lord of peace in the wind and the stillness.

"Grandpa," Kurtis said.

He turned just slightly and laid his eyes on his daughter, who looked hard and cold. "Whatcha' want, honey?" he said.

"I think it's okay if Grandma tries my bike," he said. "But maybe you ought to buy her one that's for her."

"We can do that, sweetheart," he told his grandson.

"But it's okay if she tries it. She'll probably like it," the boy said. "It's got three speeds."

"You're kidding," Wilf said.

"I got a horn too, for beeping."

"For beeping, huh?" Wilf said.

"It goes *real* fast," Kurtis said.

"Maybe too fast for Grandma," he said to his grandson.

"May-be," the boy said.

Wilf Staab had prayed before in his life. In Vietnam, often enough. And when Eleanor had some female problems Doc Beckering had to explain in a tone of voice that made him worry far more than the words. Sometimes in church—often enough for Janna and Craig—and the kids too, in the middle of it of all this darkness.

But here he was, going uphill in the darkness with just the faintest glimpse of day's end over the mountains west, and in his mind the words of his grandson who was starting to do what all of us want to do, he thought, what all of us try often enough: hide—starting already at five years old, the kind of dumping people try when they can't bring themselves to think about what it is that stands so directly and awfully in front of them. It's in all of us, he thought, me too. We all do it.

And that's why he prayed what he did in the darkness, one little sentence to a God a man or a woman almost *had* to believe in. Inside his head, with nothing above him in the bright and clear desert sky, not even the roof of his fishing truck, he said, "Good Lord, make me please a whole lot better than I am."

It was almost thirty hours of driving, and he still wasn't tired. For an old mason with shot shoulders, he thought that wasn't all bad. But he knew that sooner or later, Janna would want to talk and once again the good Lord would have to give him words to say it all just right.

Playing Through

Once, only once in my life did I ever stand close enough to my father to talk to him, even though the two of us lived almost side-by-side in a town so small there is no hiding. I've even heard him preach now and then. It's odd to listen to him, to hear him talk so openly about sin and redemption when his own unacknowledged son sits right in front of him—south side, maybe seven or eight rows back, where Jane and I and the kids always sit.

The first time I heard him preach I felt almost evil, sin's own word-made-flesh in a coat and tie not fifty feet from the pulpit. I wondered—I really did—how he could stand up there and preach with me in the pew. But he came back to our little church after that first Sunday, he returned maybe six or seven times even though he knew I'd be there. He came back, and I always assumed that by returning and standing up in front again he was telling me that what he said from the pulpit was the living word in his heart, his own testimony. If he wouldn't have found himself forgiven, I don't think he could have returned.

But I have every reason to hate a father who is not a father, a man who, with my mother, was an adulterer 32 years ago, a lay-preacher who could, without flinching, stand right in front of a son he never touched and bring the gospel of love to a church full of believers.

Only once did I ever speak to him, even though Jane and I have lived here, the town where I grew up, for almost ten years. Two years ago it happened—October, one of those last warm days that comes like a blessing. The two of us decided to take a couple hours off and put in what might well have been the last round of golf of the year. We called in for a tee-time and when we got there, the place was busy.

The kid in the pro shop had no clue. When we got inside, he just pointed behind me and said, "You mind if an extra twosome tags along, Jarred?"

I half-turned and looked directly into the face of the man who fathered me. A pall came over that man that turned him white as marble, white as salt, Lot's wife's white—that's the way I've thought of it since, my father as Lot's wife turned to an ashen pillar by this unforeseen flashback to the Sodom of his own life.

"I told them you wouldn't mind, Jarred," the kid says.

What could I say? It was a marriage made in heaven.

We played a round of golf together–some man I didn't know, Jane and I, and a local lay-preacher, a retired businessman whose DNA reads pretty much like my own. That day on the course we were our own forced marriage.

Every drive he hit was middle-of-the-fairway and not a club length over 175 yards. He was never in trouble, never took a chance over water, and on the one occasion he went in the sand, came out as if he'd been practicing all afternoon. Around the greens he was almost perfect, chipping almost professionally, rarely missing a putt under ten feet. I don't believe he could have played better golf.

I don't know my birth father, other than what he's spoken from the pulpit. For my own first eighteen years I lived in the same town, assuming the angry man in whose house I was raised was the man who'd fathered me. But I discovered the truth when I went to Oregon to live with my mother. The night she told me, she was drunk, but that was not unusual. I was 20 then, and Jane had come into my life like a great new song, a woman whose belief in God made any ordinary day into a carnival. I wanted to marry her, I said. Jane wanted to marry me. That's why I wanted to speak to Mom.

Who knows what impulse put my mother up to telling me the truth. Maybe it was a need to confess after all those years; maybe it was a warning about marriage. Who knows why she told me, but she did, remorselessly, in a story that tumbled out like drink from an upturned glass. In those years I lived with her, I found my mother in one way at least to be not unlike the man she'd left behind on the prairie—both of them steeped in bitterness. Perhaps my mother and the man who raised me took on the burden of bitterness and anger that might have otherwise come to me. She left him when I was four years old, but neither of them ever saw a dawn again after I was born. It was all darkness.

When my father died, I inherited the house the two of us had lived in on the edge of town, a place with a barn and chicken coop and a scattering of other buildings where my he had sometimes tried to make a living, and that's when Jane and I came back. My art wasn't making us rich in Oregon, and Jane thought it something of an adventure to live in a place this infinitesimal on the yawning face of a prairie landscape she didn't believe until we pulled up here in our old Travelall.

The truth is, I came back to Stockbridge healed in so many ways, some of that accomplished by my mother's late-night account of the truth of her adultery and my birth. She made the man I'd thought of as my father understandable to me, wronged as he had been early in their relationship: the man had raised an only child, a rebellious kid who never was his really, a living, breathing result of his wife's philandering. He deserved more credit than I'd ever given him.

And I came back to Stockbridge a believer, even though I'd grown up in a town where, as a boy, I don't think I could have named ten people other than my father who didn't go to church.

To say that Jane brought me to Christ would be only half-truth. She only lit the match that turned into a fire among the combustibles that growing up in Stockbridge gave my soul. She was the messenger of the good news.

We came back to Stockbridge because I'd inherited a farmhouse and scattering of buildings, and grove of dying elms that like so much of my life had to be cut down and disposed of. We came back to a town on the prairie that I'd never really thought about much until I'd lived in place where you can't see the sky, where the sun shines only occasionally, where, oddly enough, the endless succession of fast food places made me yearn for the long shadows of a yellowing prairie sunset in November.

What I'm saying is we didn't come back to Stockbridge to find my real father. That day on the golf course, thrown together as we were, was the first time I'd ever been close to the man my mother had named as her accomplice at a time in his life when he was only a little older than I am today. That day on the golf course, once Jane saw what had happened, she clung to me as if we were just-marrieds, her hand in the crook of my arm as we walked to the first tee. She's not one for public displays of affection, but that afternoon she tended my emotions as if they were hers.

All afternoon we watched that old man's half-swing send Xerox-like drives down the straight-and-narrow. All afternoon, when he talked at all, he spoke to me in golf quips—"kitty litter" for sand traps, "Nottingham" for the few trees that line this prairie course. "Keeps you humble," he mumbled on the fourth hole, when he missed the only gimme putt he didn't nail. He could have been playing with a stranger.

I've seen him forever, it seems. Even when I was a kid, an angry kid, I thought of him as old. But today, retired, it seems very strange to think of him as some horny, wandering husband. Fifty years after Auschwitz, it's hard to look at some eighty-year-old Ukrainian with folds in his cheeks and no hair and think of him as a head-basher worthy only of the gallows. My birth father may well have been barrel-chested three decades ago, but today he's paunchy and his shoulders fall inward. Beneath his chin, flesh hangs loosely, and his eyes squint constantly from the sheer fleshy weight of his eyelids.

I spoke to him only once that one day on the golf course, even though all afternoon we bantered golf chatter. After a wicked slice on the seventh hole, I hit a three-wood that came to rest in the middle of the fairway about ten yards from his third shot, but I told myself I wasn't going to speak to him–I was going to make him say something, anything. He was, after all, my father. We had to talk, really. We were thrown together again, alone. Jane was fifty yards away.

"The word is," he said, being nice, "that you and the missus are doing real well with stained glass."

I nodded.

"It's different, isn't it? —man making his living like that out here where rich people'r scarce as hen's teeth?"

"Don't sell much to locals," I said, pulling out the wedge.

"People say you do beautiful work," he told me.

I took a couple practice swings. "You ought to come by," I told him.

"Maybe so," he said, then waited as I lined up beside the ball. I had every reason in the world to boot that shot, to hit behind it and duff it halfway to the green. But I didn't. I swung gently and the ball came up with perfect loft, bounced on the green, and scurried up to within ten feet of the hole.

"You're putting the pressure on an old man," he said, already swinging his club. He played it like most retired gents. What might have looked like a squib bounced first twenty yards in front of the green, but ran up as if it had eyes for the cup and came to rest inside my ball. "Thing about this game," he said, throwing back the club, "is sometimes you get so lucky you keep coming back for more pain." It was a joke, meant as a joke, like everything else he said that day.

"Kind of like life," I said. "Isn't that the way it is?"

For a fleeting second he looked at me out of the corner of his eyes and something fell away—the old duffer pose was gone, and he stared measuringly, his forehead drawn as if he were looking at something he never dared see before. "Don't *have* to be," he said, dead serious. "Pain in life doesn't *have* to be."

"That a preacher talking, or a golfer or what?" I said.

He looked at me as if the reason I'd said that was written on my face. "That's the gospel truth," he said. And then he turned and walked away, pulling his cart behind.

A couple minutes of silence later, he was eight feet from the hole and he nailed the putt—bang!

*

"I can't believe it," Jane said when we were back in the car. "He didn't say a word, did he? In all that time, it was nothing but jokes and polite conversation. Maybe he doesn't know—"

"He knows," I told her. "I know very well he knows."

"How?"

"By his *not* talking," I said. "By the look on his face when he saw me in the pro shop. By the way he steeled himself. By the way nothing got in."

"'Got in'?" she asked.

"Inside him. Nothing. He kept it all away—anything of substance."

"I don't know how he can do it," she said, looking out over the empty road in front of us. "My goodness, you're his flesh-and-blood."

"Am I?" I said.

"Of course you are. There's part of you that's absolutely his, part of you that you can't lose."

"Maybe it's over for him," I said. "Maybe it's put behind him."

"Jerrid," she said, "you're not behind him. This afternoon you were right there in front of him. You can't put behind what's still in front."

I have so many reasons to hate the man, really. I wish we could have talked. I would have liked to know how he could put together such a sturdy game of golf when I was lucky to get off one half-decent shot per hole. What did he feel like when he got back in his pick-up? Did his heart creep up in his throat the way mine did? Did he cry? Did he close his eyes and pray, like he does in the pulpit? How could he play through?

"I don't care," Jane said, "I don't understand it. My goodness," she said again, "we are fearfully and wonderfully made."

"Why do you say that?" I asked her.

"How do you explain us? How do you explain him?" she said. "We're miracles in a way–mysteries–*X-Files*, all of us."

You get up above the valley where the golf course lies and you see town lying on the vast horizon in a darker shade of green, a floppy beret` on the spread of open prairie only occasionally shadowed by farm groves.

"Only God can love us," I told her.

She laughed. "That's not true," she said, reaching over for my shoulder.

The man I've come to call my father preached a time or two in our church after that, and I shook hands with him on my way out. But he never showed up at our studio like I asked him to, and the times that I saw him after that awkward golf match were few and far between—now and then in a supper club, once or twice picking up groceries, occasionally finishing up a round of golf.

Jane and I have this stained glass business that's finally making it. I've got clients all over the country, many of them with money enough to buy every last business in town, even the Co-op. These clients want stained glass—for their lavish estates, for their gambling casinos, for their posh restaurants—and they think it quaint to trek out here to this prairie nowhere, where they know of an artist—they call me an *artist*—who makes stained glass show pieces for their ostentation.

Jane and I work together every day. She's better with her hands than I am. Once I get an order, I sketch out a plan, a dream about color, and the two of us put it together slowly. The old barn I inherited from the man who pretended he was my father has become a studio where we make our living. We live in the very home I spent too much of life despising.

My art—my craft—is a talent I gained from my mother, a woman who made her own jewelry since the time she left the prairie and tried to find something to love in Oregon, love she claimed she'd never found in that backward place where she claimed hypocrisy was a epidemic. She thought of herself as the woman of the scarlet letter, vintage 1962.

I have something, at least, of them both, I guess.

I am 34 years old, one of the elderly of Generation X, a child of neglect and brokenness. I have three parents, only one of whom–this cold-blooded golfer–seemed at all able to cope with my own adulterous conception.

And he died last week. No one called me, but word gets around in so small a place as this. He died in his sleep, people say, peacefully.

Peacefully.

"You should go," Jane told me. She was doing a Tiffany lamp just then because it's nearly Christmas season and we can move some little things if they're sitting around the studio when clients come in. Her hands were dirty, but I love the way her rolled-up sleeves ride her forearms. I like the way her hair falls from whatever pins she puts it in. I like her cheeks. I like her silence. I like her words. "There's a kind of end to it now," she told me, brushing her chin with the back of her hand. "If you go to the funeral, you can put it all away."

"I don't need a ceremony," I told her.

"We all do." She hunched her shoulders. "Like I said, it's kind of an end."

"Kind of end is right"—

"I'm not being funny," she said. "I mean it. It's always that way, isn't it? Death. Any death. There's a kind of end to things here—even with him." She turned her head just slightly, as if there were some high-pitched sound coming to her somehow. "Even with you," she said. "Just like his wife—it's time to say goodbye."

I pulled the cap back from my head and rubbed the soles of my hands through my eyes. "You'll come too?"

She nodded.

No one in that church would have thought it strange to see me at his funeral. He was well known, a lay-preacher, a fine man, a community leader. Thirty-some years ago he was also an adulterer who fathered a child born of a mother who eventually flew the coop and thereby, to these people, committed a sin most unforgivable in abandoning her child. Few know that, or, if they do, they don't say it.

Only three people in the entire world know the whole story now: I am one, and Jane is another. No one who came to the funeral read anything in my attending that funeral other than admiration for what most of Stockbridge would call a fine, fine man.

Did you ever notice that passages from the Bible sound more like the voice of God at funerals than any other time in our lives? In this town there are some of the folks who attend funerals the way others seek revivals, to participate in the intense moments funerals offer—the moment the grieving family walks in together, the moment the pastor singularly addresses them, the moment he reads the God-breathed power of a passage like Psalm 90, and the closing, finally, of the casket. Maybe my mother was right—we're not all far from New England.

To me, the funeral was uplifting. No hymn satisfies quite as fully as "Peace Like a River." We sat two rows from the back, right side, alone, the attention in the place focused upon my father's wife, who is the third of the only three people who know the whole story, and I sang with the others, not so much for her as some do, but for myself, "It is well with my soul." You know the piece.

She'd lost him unexpectedly. Men far older than he was live on much longer than they'd like. There are four children, my half-brothers and sisters, none of whom live around here, none of them know me. As the service ended, his wife walked up the aisle to the back of the church on the arm of her eldest daughter, a woman who looked two decades older than Jane.

The rest of us left slowly, row after row, and the whole time I waited in that pew I sat there imagining myself a medical student, probe in hand, going through my father's mind, trying to locate a picture of me, an artifact, maybe some trace of regret, of sadness, at least something of his sin made flesh. There are really so many reasons for me to hate him.

Not until I pulled on my coat did I decide not to go to cemetery. So much of that man's life, after all, was never mine. I pulled on my gloves and swung the scarf around my neck before closing up the buttons of my coat, and I stepped outside, Jane holding my hand.

The procession going to the grave yard was already lined up, hearse in front, still positioned where it was when the pallbearers trucked the casket from the church and into its open maw. Directly behind it stood the family car, a Lincoln. There is little lawn in front of that church on that side, and the only means to the parking lot is a sidewalk that ran directly past that car.

We were legion. Lots of people attended that funeral, but I did not drop my eyes as I walked past that Lincoln, and I saw his wife in the middle of the back seat, her shoulders cushioned by children on either side. I saw her as clearly as I did her husband's ashen face that day in the pro shop when a foursome was decided by some act of fate. I looked into her eyes for just a moment, wanting nothing more than the kind of nod that would tell me the whole story. Maybe I wanted to be thanked–I don't know. Maybe all I wanted from her was some bit of my identity, some acknowledgement of the truth.

What she gave me was a stare, something dazed that could well have been over her face from medication or the sheer weight of too much horror too fast for an old woman and wife suddenly bereft of a husband. What she gave me was a stare, and then, almost imperceptibly, a wave that came and went with a suddenness that I believe only Jane and I ever noted. But I saw it, four weak fingers no more than chin-high aimed exclusively at me, one of dozens of people right there on the front sidewalk of church. She waved. I saw it, and so did my wife.

We live in a place where people wave constantly, not so much out of friendliness, I think, as a kind of defense. If you don't, people think you're uppity or harboring a grudge. Jane couldn't get used to it. "I don't even know the people," she said to me years ago. "Doesn't matter," I told her. But this was not something perfunctory or defensive. It was only a moment of acknowledgement of our mutual suffering. I will likely never speak to her, but I could never thank her enough.

We got in the car and drove away out into the country, into the farmland, where this time of year the whole barren country waits for a blanket of snow to cover its nakedness. But I didn't steer us home. We drove east, then south, so slowly the gravel roads cracked like frozen snow beneath my tires. Eventually I turned west, crossed the highway a mile out of town, and kept going until I came to a crossroads where we could see the cemetery far above. I pulled the car to the side of the road maybe a half-mile from the place where a hoarded of black coats were huddled on the frosted grass around a canvas windbreak.

I told Jane I wondered if people chose hills for cemeteries because the distance to heaven is closer than it would be from river valleys or flat land.

"That may be it," she said, "but why the stones, then? – Why the flowers? It's a place of memory." She reached over again and took my arm. "Why not look up to it?"

I am not my father's child alone—a one-time philanderer, a man carrying secrets stoically to his grave; and I am not my mother's child either—an alcoholic, an angry, bitter woman who faced more darkness from her unloving husband than she could take. But neither am I his son, a man predisposed given so deeply to spite that all his days were lived in shadows his own displeasure raised against the sun. That's what I told my wife.

"But you could be," she told me. We both know children of alcoholics, children of abusers. We both know ritual and cyclical patterns of behavior.

The two of us sat alone in the warmth of our Travelall at my father's graveyard service, beneath a limitless hazy sky of December blue, down the dusky road from a cluster of stooped mourners, my wife and I, whispering our own psalms of praise.

Paternity

Somewhere today a woman named Cassandra Something-or-other is telling a little different story, I'm sure, because she was rich and likely still is.

What do I remember of her? Her hair–the way she turned her face up into the brisk, beach sun and swept the long bronzed bangs across her cheeks. The way she laughed, always hard and full, embarrassingly sometimes–for me, not her–and the way she never giggled, even though she was only sixteen. The sharp fortitude of her eyes confronting yours and never once backing down. I remember her body very well–and her tan, both where it was and where it wasn't. Her face, really–the exact shape of her nose and the thickness of her eyebrows, even her lips–has gone from my memory, but a part of her will never go, the ever-urging boldness that knew no fear.

The fall of her sophomore year she and her mother moved, all year round, into her parents_ cottage on the lake. She was what we called "lake people." I was a townie. Her father owned a Chicago company that turned out fifty fiberglass boats per day. My father milked thirty-five cows. Twice she'd been to Europe. I'd been to Indiana three times to Bible Camp. She was going to college in Vermont, she said, because she hated Chicago, where she'd lived for her first fifteen years.

We were both sixteen. I was an athlete, tall and muscular from years of farm work, and blond, like a beach bum, from the burning sun and long hours in the alfalfa fields that still lay like storybook meadows between Easton and the woods that belt the lakeshore. I wanted her all right, but she just wanted. That was the difference between Cassie and normal Easton girls. They never really wanted. Cassie did—sincerely and truly.

Once I told her how—when I was a boy—we'd seen a train flatten a penny we'd laid on the track. A half hour later she stood, holding a handful of unruly hair to keep it out of her face, while only ten feet away a huge freight exploded by. The miniature football I'd hung on a chain from my rearview mirror swayed in the lurches of the coal cars across those ties, and I was in the car fifty feet away; but she never raised her eyes from the spot on the steel where she'd planted a nickel herself.

I wasn't really Gary Dirks to her. I was merely the boy she wanted. Eight times we made love. I could probably still list them, by place and degree of success, in order. And we really didn't quit each other, at least not until the next summer, when she became pregnant and went back to Chicago to have our baby.

She had no desire to marry me, the son of an Easton Hollander, a small dairyman. So she finished high school in Chicago, I suppose, and I never heard from her again, just as she had promised. When I say she left Easton, I don't mean that her parents forced her to return to Chicago. She simply determined herself that she would leave, then told her mother of her plans. Back then I thought of Cassia's having free will in the theological sense my father talked about "free will"–as the opposite of being predestined for salvation, almost as sin.

Yesterday, I sat on a crowded curb in my hometown as a Dutch Festival parade marched up from the memory of my sixteenth summer in Easton, one float after another, the Lions Club's old black and gold, papier-mâché feline still mounted on the same crepe-papered hayrack, First Presbyterian's same black Bible open to the same John 3:16. Only the faces of the queen and her court had changed; even their Dutch costumes seemed hand sewn replicas of what I remembered. My children were off on the Tilt-a-Whirl and the Ferris wheel because a silly, small-town parade doesn't entertain ten-year-olds who have been brought up on cartoon excesses. So I sat there alone and watched another parade too: a score of Easton high school kids dressed down for the sun, performing for each other. And I remembered who I was back then, sixteen years ago.

I remembered Cassie and our child and my own father, who yesterday was out baling hay somewhere, just as he was during the Dutch Festival in town that summer I became a father myself. We'd had a New Holland baler for four years already and developed a list of farmer-customers long enough to call ourselves the Dirks_ family custom balers—my two older brothers, Andy and Darrell, and myself. The three of us usually set things up and took turns working in the mow or in the field; then there was the boss, my father, of course, who always finished the milking at home before getting out to join us; and my little brother Jesse, eleven-years-old maybe, who usually drove the wagons back and forth and loaded bales on the elevator. Three cuts we made some years; some years only two.

Nothing remarkable happened the afternoon Cassie and I told my parents about her being pregnant. Cassia's mother was there too, the collar of her lavender blouse lying open, tastefully, over her tanned chest. When I remember now how strange that woman looked in our farm house—with all our fans churning up the air—I can see in the collar of that silk blouse what it was that determined, finally, my father's nodding silence: he didn't know how to talk to a woman who looked like she'd just stepped from a television screen. My mother, in her kitchen smock, smiled the way good women can when they have to; but my father sat and listened, his hands folded in his lap as if he were in church.

Cassie controlled the conversation. It was her style to talk, to reason out what must be done, and she did, with such coolness that she disarmed my mother's usually hair-triggered emotions. She explained how she knew it was Easton tradition to marry a couple of kids at a time like this, but how that would be foolish, neither of us even seventeen and neither of us really seriously in love. She told my mother how she was going to move back to Chicago and have the baby there, and how she didn't blame me for the baby because it wasn't my fault alone any more than it was hers. It was, simply, what had happened, she said.

At that point my mother reached for her handkerchief.

"Of course, we expect to be able to cover the entire financial picture," her mother threw in, as if it were the line that Cassie had allowed her to say.

At five, my father, taking his cue from the tolling of the clock in the family room, went out to the barn, sensing, I'm sure, that nothing more could be said anyway.

If I'd scour my high school annual I could come up with two or three other Easton girls who got pregnant that summer, but the story that unfolded in those cases would have been completely different. Once the news was out, Cassie packed her bags quickly for Chicago; as a result, the elders from my church never did visit with us together, as was the custom with the other shotgunned couples who'd violated the seventh commandment. Since she was already gone, they visited me alone, three of them, all men; and once they had nudged the word sin into and out of the conversation, we spent the rest of the night talking about football, my senior year upcoming.

I never saw Cassie again, nor the child–wherever he or she may be–if, in fact, that child exits. Cassie had money like I'd never seen. That was 1970, before Roe vs. Wade, but the Mikklesons had the kind of money that could pay for illegality.

Some summer nights a few years later, when I was home from college, I drove slowly down the lake road past their home late at night, maybe once a week or so. I'm not sure what drew me back so frequently to that path through the birch just a couple hundred feet off the lakefront–lust maybe, but I don't think that's the whole reason. Maybe I wanted to know that what had happened was all real.

But what I remember best about that summer is what happened after Cassie and her mother made their afternoon visit to our dairy–what I saw that night in the barn, and what my father said the next day, when he finally opened up.

He caught me once, maybe a year before, beating a cow with a hoe. I don't remember the provocation anymore, but a milk cow, like a wife or a sister or a brother, can make you feel that bloody kind of hate you can feel only for those you live with, day-in, day-out. He came up from behind and grabbed me, lifted me off the cement and kept me up there until he'd stopped my thrashing.

"You ever do that again, Gary," he said, "and so help me I'll use that hoe on you."

That's all he said about it, ever.

When Cassie and her mother left late that afternoon, I went out to the barn, maybe a half hour after my father picked up and left in silence. I pulled on my boots just outside the parlor and unlatched the door. I was young then, cocky. I figured I'd take my licks and have it over. But I found him beating a cow that night, whacking away, the milking machine lying awkwardly in the gutter like some overturned turtle. He had a dowel he'd picked up somewhere, thick as his finger, and he was thrashing that cow like I'd never seen him do before.

When he saw me standing there where the rest of the cows were already stanchioned, he stopped, frozen in the act, a vacant, stunned look on his face. We both knew that nothing needed to be said, so we milked beside each other all night long and never spoke a word. I felt almost excused, as if what I'd done with Cassie was lost in some big harvest of sin.

The next morning we were out baling hay at the Trillian place, an old farm with hundreds of acres of land and a sprawling, ramshackle barn with 1904 painted below the point of the eaves.

Today, the baler my father bought is obsolete because people say a crew of five or six makes baling hay too labor-intensive. Today, with the right kind of equipment, one man can do all the haying and never leave the air-conditioned comfort of his cab. Back then, haying employed our entire family, locked us up in dusty mows, forced us to gulp ice-cold lemonade from a common-cup canning jar, to work long, hot hours in stagnant air, thick with dust, and talk to each other, even if we may not have wanted to.

When my father came on the job that morning, we'd already started up. I was stacking bales on the wagon when I saw his pickup roll into the yard. My brother Andy was driving the baler, while old man Trillian himself shuttled the first load back to the barn where he and little Jesse unloaded. In a matter of minutes, half hour maybe, Darrell rode out on the empty wagon and told me Dad wanted me to work with him in the barn.

My brothers hadn't said much to me that morning. They knew what had happened the night before, but on the ride out to Trillian's I'd found a corner in the back of the wagon and they let me be. Maybe they were disappointed in me, I don't know. Maybe they were jealous. Whatever they felt, they didn't say much. Maybe they felt as I did–it was all water over the dam. The way I saw it, Cassie was leaving. Now it was her problem.

My father is a tall, gaunt man with very dry hair and proud features, a wide nose that, come summer, reddens almost daily. His arms are long, and his hands carry muskmelons as if they were softballs. He resembles the picture we have of his grandfather, the North Sea sailor who, eighty years ago, decided to leave the

Netherlands and cut a life for himself and his family from uncut Dakota grasslands.

My father has mellowed in the years that have passed since that summer. He laughs now as he watches his own grandchildren play on the rope swing he hung, not four years ago, from the maple I remember as a sapling. Back then, with three teenage boys and six children in all, with thirty-five milk cows, with all of that life riding the back of the cold and dreary lakeshore seasons, he seemed to me to be driven. I remember unforeseen spurts of temper during harvest, nervousness in unexplained silences during early spring planting. Whole nights passed in October when he didn't speak a word to my mother or to us.

Although he was a man to be feared then, it would be wrong to say that I was ever afraid of my father. He was to be feared the way he himself talked about fearing God. Each of us, I think, lived in a kind of awe of him. Darrell, the oldest, still wrestles him: if Dad says Darrell shouldn't use herbicides, Darrell claims he'll go bankrupt if he doesn't. Andy simply follows Dad. He's learned to live with him the way a good Marine feels comfort in a well-defined chain of command. I don't claim to know about myself.

"You know," he said to me that day when I'd climbed up in the mow beside him, "I always thought it would be Darrell and Gloria, the way they neck. I didn't think it would be you."

Little Jesse was loading the bales on the elevator that poked its nose into a square door maybe twenty feet off the ground. Trillian was helping him. We were putting hay up in the corners of the east loft, and the air was hot, full of chaff and dust, even though it wasn't past ten or eleven in the morning.

"We're all capable of it," he said. "I'm not throwing the first stone either."

He pointed me over to the place where he'd been packing. "Watch out for those kittens there," he said. His stacking had uprooted four of them, gray ones–farm cats–certainly no more than a month old, from their nest, so he'd put them up beside a rafter that he likely didn't mean to cover. The end of the yellow elevator, anchored with twine down to the wall, protruded from the open door behind him, sunlight cutting through the maze of dust in perfect geometric shafts.

"You know you shouldn't have done it," he said, not meaning it as a question.

I nodded.

When he didn't hear me reply, he looked straight up at me.

"Yes," I told him.

"Our bodies are the temple of the Lord," he said.

I really didn't feel any less healthy having made love eight times. It didn't seem somehow like a desecration.

When a bale came up the elevator, it fell, end first, down to the floor where it grazed off the edge of another set deliberately below, then flipped over completely, landing flat, strings up, four, maybe five feet closer to the spot where we were trying to fill in the last of the holes in that corner of the mow. He'd grab them from the spot where they'd finally come to rest and heave them at me. Jesse was sending them up plenty fast.

"I've been thinking for hours," he said, "and I just don't know what to say to you that you don't already know."

I didn't talk back. I was sorry for letting them down the way I did, but Cassie wasn't really a girl I'd marry anyway, I thought. I'd miss her. I knew I would. But I didn't love her, not love like you're supposed to, I thought. Besides, she really wasn't even of us. She was "lake people." And she was leaving.

"Slow down, Jesse," he yelled down the open hole. "We're finishing up up here."

He motioned with his arm for me to climb up and take the bales from him when he picked them off the floor. His was the heavy work; mine was simply tedious: fitting them into what spaces remained.

"The church calls it a sin," he said.

"I know it," I told him.

"I don't know if it's a bigger sin if it happened a hundred times, or a little one if it happened just once," he said, "but you and this girl, how often did you do it?"

I don't know why I said what I did, but I told him it had happened four times. "But she let me do it, Dad," I told him.

"Every time. She told me that it was okay, that nothing would happen."

"You and Adam," he said. He picked up a bale and heaved it up to me off his knee. I was standing on a ledge of bales maybe four feet above him.

"Well, you saw her," I told him.

"Sure I did."

"She let me."

"Slow down, Jesse," he yelled again. Bales were piling up after flipping over the end as if they were riding a waterfall.

He pulled his handkerchief out and wiped his face. "So you just go and do whatever that thing you got in your pants says? —Is that it?" He stopped and stared at me, bales still falling heavily to the floor.

I threw one in a hole without looking up at all. But I didn't talk.

"Does it say somewhere in the Bible that it's all just fine and dandy if the girl says yes? Is that a verse you read somewhere?"

I was up high, I remember. I reached up and scraped away cobwebs so thick with dust that they could have passed for yarn. But he stayed there at my feet, staring. I wouldn't look at him.

He turned around and grabbed for another bale. That's when I said, "Any guy would have done it, and you know it."

"Does that make it right?" he said, shoving another one up at me.

I twisted around, keeping my feet straight beneath me as I picked up the bale and swung it into a hole at the corner of the roofline.

"What's the big deal?" I said. "By football season it'll be all over anyway."

I'm not sure where that came from.

"Football season," my father said, in a tone without emotion, as if he were repeating it in order to get me to verify that what I'd said actually came from my lips.

"That's what I said," I told him.

His face turned suddenly into some fierce mask. "It'll all be over, will it?" he said, laughing in a biting, mature way that I'd never heard him laugh before, as if I wasn't his own boy.

Behind him the bales kept falling all over the spaces where he could walk. He twisted around quickly, as if he had forgotten what he was about. He scrambled down two levels of bales to get to the window, then dug his knees into the hay to look outside. "Slow down, Jesse—didn't you hear me?" he yelled, and he grabbed the end of the elevator and shook it. He stayed there for a minute, ripped four bales from the track and stacked them, one atop the next, to keep them out of the way.

Seated over there, he had to yell for me to hear. "You think it'll all be over, do you?" he said. "Just like that—like the mumps. You think it'll all go away, just like that. Like a sore knee, is that it?"

"What?" I said. "She'll be gone. She's rich. You saw her old lady. She'll take care of the whole business."

The floor at the end of the elevator was cluttered with bales. He pulled himself up from his knees, grabbed the end of the elevator, and twisted himself around it; but his foot slipped in a crack, and he twisted his back when he couldn't keep his balance, finally falling to all fours. Just like that, like a slap in the face with an open hand, another bale came off the end and slammed to the floor over his twisted foot.

He came up swearing under his breath, something he rarely did, and he grabbed that elevator and twisted it, wrestled it loose from the knot Andy must have tied to anchor it, the chain jangling like loose bells, then turned it completely upside down, dumping every last bale off the track and to the ground between the barn and the wagon. "Now slow down!" he yelled again at Jesse.

"You don't have to lose your temper," I said.

"You shut up," he said, pointing back at me. "You talk like a child–it'll all be over–" he said. "It's no big deal at all because once you make a touchdown nobody will remember."

Anger and hurt twisted his mouth and narrowed his eyes, pouring out in something close to tears. "We're talking about life here. Don't you understand that–or is all you care about getting laid?"

I never heard my father use that kind of language.

"Life," he said, and he put both hands down on a row of bales and climbed up several levels, lifting himself to the nest of kittens he'd laid at the beam. He grabbed a kitten from the pile that he'd found up there, took it in his huge hand and held it towards me like some circus magician, the kitten's round head protruding between his thumb and forefinger, the rest of its body in his fist, small and gray with long fur. He raised it higher and higher towards me, then jerked down suddenly, as if he were snapping his fingers, as if he were a kid snapping a lead pencil in half. When he opened his hand, the kitten was perfectly dead.

I couldn't believe what he'd done.

He didn't say anything just then. He looked at me and tossed the kitten across the mow somewhere. If his eyes could have spoken, they would have explained everything, but his eyes were vacant. He just stood there and stared, almost as if I could be next.

"Dad–" I said.

"You two made a child," he said, "not a kitten."

And just then Jesse came up the ladder, almost crying himself. "I tried to get that old guy to slow down, but he just kept on going," he said. "I tried."

"That's what you made," my father said, pointing at Jesse. "And who's going to be nice to him–who's going to dry up his tears, Gary? You going to be there?"

Two years ago, I was divorced. I could give you a hundred reasons why, but none of them would be any good really. Anyway,

I see my two kids on weekends, and I take them places but you get tired of amusement parks and malls. So I took them to the Dutch Festival in Easton yesterday, a half-day's ride north of Chicago, where we live.

Today I'm a teacher, special ed, in the schools there. My students are kids who don't understand why it's important to show up for work in the morning if you want to keep a job. And every year I get new ones, a new crop of sixteen-year-olds. This year I will too. And I wonder sometimes if I'd recognize that one of Cassie and me, the one I never saw. Maybe it was a girl.

Somewhere, I imagine, Cassandra Whoever-she's-married-to is telling her story too, and it's probably not at all the same.

But I couldn't help thinking when I was sitting there yesterday on the curb, when I saw all those Dutch kids around town, all those preening girls and the boys with the developing shoulders, that somewhere someplace there's this tall, gaunt, half-Dutch, sixteen-year-old, who could just as well be up in a stuffy haymow somewhere with my father, wearing out overalls by hoisting bales on his knee, his face sticky with sweat and chaff, and sometimes talking, sometimes talking.

What He Needed To Say

Wednesday—bacon, lettuce, and tomato. Soon enough, he'd have to throw the tomatoes away if he didn't use them. Thursday—potpies; the kids loved them, even though he always felt guilty because they were so easy. That left Friday, the weekend—take the girls out for pizza. Nick would be gone to soccer or something with the guys. Ben looked down at the list and told himself he hadn't done a half-bad job being mom.

In South Africa, where Lynda was on sabbatical, it was late winter, even though back here in the States only a few days of summer were left before the kids would head out to school. The advantage of her studying South African literature was that she could spend her summers in Pretoria, when it was winter down there, the schools in full swing until Christmas. Afrikaans fiction was a species of literature she had in her genes she said, being Dutch Calvinist herself, like the Afrikaners.

Right now she'd be sitting at some desk in an apartment he'd only pictured from Lynda's careful e-mail descriptions. She'd have a sweater thrown over her shoulders, her reading glasses on her nose, her face slightly upturned. He remembered how, some mornings in bed, she'd wrap her shoulders in her bathrobe to keep away a chill. Odd, he thought, how images like that could come to him at the strangest times. In the middle of some patient's recitation of this or that ailment, his mind would suddenly flash to their bedroom, where he'd watch her twist her shoulders while reaching behind her to fasten her bra. Some nights he'd dream about her walking into the bedroom as if she'd never left.

He put down the grocery list and picked up his father's new book—memories of the Nazi occupation in the Netherlands, of the starving winter when cats were passed off as rabbits to hungry people, a whole collection of stories he'd heard from his father in snippets throughout his childhood. He hadn't brought himself to read it through, because even browsing would force him to sympathy. His father was a tough man, tougher on his son, Ben thought, than he should have been—the war this, the war that. He let the book fall open. "My sister was released from the camp at Vught after her boyfriend was killed because the SS thought women wouldn't work for the Resistance if their husbands hadn't put them up to it. The SS didn't know my sister."

To believe Tante Aantje could ever have fought Nazis was impossible. She still lived in Holland, where she spent most of her time keeping up the garden around her modest home. Sweet Tante Antje fighting Nazis.

He raised the shade to see Nick coming up the sidewalk from his car. Eleven o'clock, right on time for a Sunday night. He never knew whether to judge his son's almost perfect behavior as a measure of their success as parents, or their failure. Nick loved being at home so much that sometimes they had to shoo him out.

He put his father's book down, pulled the empty ice cream saucer from the cat's covetous eyes, and sat up as the screen door shrieked and the back steps moaned beneath his son's footfalls.

"How's it going?" he asked as Nick came up the stairs.

Nick stood there as if in a daze, the long pipes of the doorbell chimes in front of him. Lynda had been gone only six weeks, but already she wouldn't recognize him, their son having grown a foot, it seemed.

"There's some of that ice cream you like—"Death by Chocolate," he told him, snickering, but Nick barely shrugged his shoulders. "Something the matter?" Ben said.

With the kind of jerking motion that had become obsessive with him since he'd parted his hair down the middle, he shook both ends back behind his ears, but never moved his eyes from the chimes, didn't move an inch.

"Nick," he said, "something happen or what?"

At that the kid turned slowly, as he were feeling guilty about the smears over his cheeks, the tracks of tears.

"What is it?" he said.

"Quinn's girl, Shannon," he said, grabbing one of the long pipes as if he could rip it from the wall. "You didn't hear?"

"Hear what?"

"What happened?"

"No," Ben said.

Nick brought a fist to his face as if to cover a cough. "She's dead," he said. "Got killed tonight—"

"Killed?" Ben said.

"A train. On Farrows Road." He pointed over his shoulder as if the intersection were right behind him. "You know that railroad crossing?"

"When?"

"Tonight."

"Just now?"

Nick raised the heels of his hands to his eyes. "Around seven." He made a spitting noise, as if trying to expel the hurt. "She must have been driving into the sun because there was no way you could miss it coming," he said, "the train I mean. How could you miss a train? —Tell me that, Dad—how could somebody miss seeing a train?"

However many tears had already been shed were not enough to cover the hurt. He looked as if he could lose it again any time.

"How's Quinn?" he said.

Nick kicked off his moccasins and slumped to the rug, kept an elbow up to support his head, legs splayed beneath him. He took a burdened breath. "A mess," he said. "He's like, torn up completely. He's a wreck." And then he cried, not audibly, not even visibly. Into his forearm. Just covered his eyes and turned away, shoulders throbbing.

Ben didn't know this Shannon, knew only that Quinn, like Nick, hadn't had much success with girls, hadn't tried either, both of them loners and proud of it. The girlfriend business had come up only in the last few weeks, after Lynda had left. Sometimes Nick laughed about his buddy, as if the thought of Quinn in a car alone with a girl was a scream.

"It's like he's not even Quinn," Nick said, rubbing his eyes. "I've never yet been to a funeral," he said. "I never thought anything could hurt somebody so bad." And then he cried again, in sobs he battled to hold back.

Ben pulled himself up from the chair but stayed on his knees and waded across the room. "I'm sorry," he said, then sat with his folded legs beneath him. He squared his back against the couch, and grabbed Nick's knee like a gearshift, just to let him know he was there. They were not the touching type, never had been. Sometimes seeing other fathers hugging their boys made him angry with his own father for passing along this iron-like reserve. He reached for Nick's shoulder. "I'm sorry," he said, "for you—and for Quinn—and for her family," he said. "That's just awful." Nothing sounded real.

Nick tried yawning his face out of distortion. "It's all I been doing is bawling," he said. "I got to quit." He shook his head as if to loosen something. "How long does it take before you stop losing it? I mean, when something like this happens, how long before you can shut off the water?"

"Why stop?" he said.

"I'm sick of it," Nick snapped. "It's like having the flu—you can't do anything about it, huh? Doesn't even pay to try."

"You been over there?"

Nick shook his head yes.

"All night?"

"Quinn should have been with her," he said. "She was going to meet him in town—taking the car," he said. "He's a mess too because he says it's all his fault—that he didn't pick her up. He says it wouldn't have happened if he wasn't playing Nintendo."

"It isn't his fault—"

"You can't tell him nothing," Nick growled. "All he does is fall apart." He pulled his knees up beneath him. "What do you say?" he said. "Everything sounds like commercials—everything."

"Just let him be," Ben said. "You got to just let him be."

"*Quinn's crazy, Dad,*" he'd told his father six weeks ago. "*Quinn's got this girl on his mind, like all the time. It's nuts.*"

"Who is this Shannon?" he said, taking hold of his son's knee. "I mean, what's her last name?"

"Timmons," he said. "She lives down there–on Fallows Road. Her parents have this place on the lake. She's a sophomore" and then, reluctantly, "*was*." He dragged his shirtsleeve across his eyes, clearing the tangles. "I wish Mom was here."

"So do I," he said. In the silence, he steered away from the cold questions, the factual stuff. This wasn't just anyone's death, after all. This was something horrible, something he remembered himself now, in the sheen of his son's own tears. He tried to come up with something sincere for Nick, something to say, something adult, but he remembered very well that there wasn't anything. He remembering being Quinn. He looked at his watch. It was after eleven, but what did curfew mean? What difference did anything make? "Whyn't you just go back, Nick?" he said. "You hear me? – You're not going to sleep anyway. Believe me. Neither is Quinn."

"It's all darkness," Nick said. "I mean, I don't see nothing in front of me–I really don't. There's this wall and it goes all the way up to heaven," he said. "I can't imagine life without Shannon– and what about Quinn, Dad?" he asked. "How bad would it be then?"

Three days and school starts, Ben thought.

"It's like nothing that ever happened to me," Nick said. "I look at Quinn and I don't know what to tell him." He raised his hands. "We just sat on his bed and bawled—"

"'We'? —"

"Freddy and Sam were there—three of us." With his thumb and fingers, Nick pinched at his forehead as if he could squeeze out the headache. "He says he loved her, Dad." His eyes lifted to the window on the other side of the room. "He keeps saying all the time how much he loved her." He pumped a fist against his leg. "Shoot, he just started going with her, a couple months—not even." He shook back his hair, stared at the ceiling. "You think he's just saying that? You really think he *loved* her?"

"Maybe he did," Ben said, "in his own way."

"*Real* love," he said, "like you and Mom?"

"That's probably what he thinks, I'm sure," Ben told him. "Especially now."

"But *is* it?" he said. "Is it really love?"

"Doesn't pay to try to tell him different," Ben said.

"Then what's he got left, Dad? —I mean it," Nick said, and he pulled himself to his knees. "Then what's Quinn got to look forward to in his life with her gone—if he really loved her?" Both hands came up to pull back his hair. "What's the sense?"

So much should be said, but couldn't, Ben thought. Nick was right. Everything that came to mind was like commercials, so much tripe. "He's got a lot, really," Ben told him. "He's got a lifetime ahead of him, Nick—believe me." Flimsy words.

He'd never told Nick about Sally, his high school girl, the whole horrible story—never thought about telling, never considered it – a death that had happened so long ago it was hard to believe he was the same human being. His girl, Sally – in a plane crash. Thirty years ago already,

"How can you say to him that there's still life ahead of him?" Nick said, pulling one leg beneath him and sitting again. "He thinks everything is done. He thinks his whole life is shot. The girl he loved is dead. What's the use?"

"Lots of life ahead of him," Ben said.

Nick pulled his fingers in and out, making a fist. "There's got to be something to tell him," he said. "There's got to be more. Shoot, Dad, you're a doctor. You deal with this stuff every day." He looked at him earnestly. "We're Christians, aren't we?"

He jerked on his son's knee, brought it down against his thigh. "Listen to this," he said. "This is what Job says, 'The Lord giveth, the Lord taketh away. Blessed be the name of the Lord.'"

"I can't tell him that—"

"I know," Ben said.

"He'd blow up," Nick said, "he would."

"I know he would—"

"Then why should I say it?"

"You don't have to *say* anything, Nick," Ben said. "You just have to be there." He squeezed his son's knee tightly. "It takes time to believe, to hear real words." What he remembered were ditties that came out of people's mouths like thin shards of glass.

"You *want* me to believe, don't you?" Nick said.

"I want you to believe it because it's true," he said. "But right now isn't the time to figure anything out. Quinn's got all he can do to just stand up—so do you." He remembered the hunger of his emptiness, a terror so alive it clawed at his soul. In love? —of course it was love. What possible good could it be to tell a kid he wasn't in love?

"Maybe I'm not making sense, Nick," he said. "I'm sorry. I should be better at this, but what I'm saying is that right now crying is okay," he said. "Take it from the doctor. I know it is."

Nick stared into his open palms.

"I know it because I lived through it myself."

Nick looked up him, wiped his eyes with the back of his hands.

"I lost this girl," he said, "just like Quinn."

"True?" he said.

"Swear to God."

"You loved her?"

"I loved her," he said, with no hesitation. "I'm sure I loved her."

The cat pranced out of the kitchen and walked beneath Nick's leg, leaving her tail up against his skin.

"You lost a girl you loved—she died like Shannon?" he said. "Got killed? —Before there was Mom?"

"Before Mom," he said, and he got to his feet, then reached down and pulled the ends of his son's long hair around his ears like Lynda might have. Sometimes Nick would come up to her and hug her for no particular reason, just hold her. Sometimes he'd lie on the couch with his head in her lap while they watched the news, Lynda taking his hair in her fingers and showing him playfully where she thought it ought to be trimmed. He reached down and slipped his hand beneath Nick's collar and held him at the base of his neck just for a moment, then pulled away and walked into the kitchen, to the freezer, the ice cream.

"You never told me that," Nick said. "You're not making this up?"

"I'm not making it up," he said.

He'd bought the ice cream for Nick, a "limited time only" flavor. Right now it would be a taste of something else, something cold, something good.

It had happened so long before the kids, before Lynda, before so much of his life that it was hard to believe the five people most precious to him today—their little girls up in bed sleeping, his son Nick, and Lynda—that all of them and all of their world came so long after Sally, after tears he once thought would never stop.

He pulled two bowls out of the cupboard and watched Nick's head turn toward him. Then he unfolded the top of the carton and searched through the drawer for the scoop. There was something unfeeling about telling another story right now, as if one-upping him. Nick had every right to his own horror. He flicked the ice cream from the spoon with his finger. Yet, maybe it was the right time now, a moment only God Almighty could plan. Not that he knew what to say. But he had a story.

"This girl I dated," he said, "she died when we were your age. Got killed. In a plane. She was killed in a plane crash in Colorado. That was years ago." He shoveled three long smooth crescents of dark chocolate into a saucer bigger than an ordinary cereal bowl, then filled another for himself. It was the kind of eating together the two of them needed. "Did you go to *her* house? —" He asked, "Shannon's?"

Nick was still rubbing his eyes. "Quinn's folks wouldn't let him go. He wanted to," he said, "but they told him, "later." That time would come. He was ticked—"

"Because he couldn't go?"

"Yeah."

"They were right. It's one thing if you're married—"

"But he loved her," Nick said. "You said it yourself."

"Sure he did," Ben said. "I'm sure he loved her." He carted the bowls into the family room, stood over his son, and held out the one with the extra scoop, made him reach for it. "Here, eat it—good for you."

Nick took the bowl. "I almost get to feeling bad about how I feel," he said. "Sometimes I think I'm hurting for Quinn more than for Shannon—I mean, Shannon's the dead one." He shrugged his shoulders. "It's not that I don't feel sorry for her—I mean, for her parents. And it's not that I don't miss her, Dad, I mean, already. I didn't know her that well, really, but I look at Quinn and it just seems like everything in him is dead—"

"It is—"

"I feel like if I'd tip him over, he'd be like that Christmas scene-thing Mom always puts on the buffet—everything's falling." He shook his head again. "Nothing you say comes out right," he said. "Your mind doesn't work. It does crazy things. You say weird things." He shook his head. "The bed was wet, Dad," he said. "Quinn's bed was wet from all the crying—shit," he said, "a bunch of guys."

"That's all right," Ben said.

And then he looked up. "You're not lying, really? —You had a girlfriend that was killed?" he said. "In a plane crash? She got killed in a plane crash?"

It hurt—the way he said it—*killed*. "Long ago," he told him, "coming home from a church project, from New Mexico. Teaching in a Bible school in a little Navajo church—"

"You were my age?" Nick said.

Ben nodded, his mouth purposely full.

"How come I never knew?"

"I never told you," he said. "Maybe I should have."

Nick half-turned and squinted at him. "You *loved* her–this girl?" Nick said. "She was some high school sweetheart?"

Ben shook his head yes.

Nick turned away. "My old man in love with somebody else," he said, stunned. "How come you never told me? –I mean, it had it to be a huge thing."

Ben could see the story grow in his son's imagination, Nick's eyes narrowing. "Coming home from some church thing?" he said. "The truth?"

He nodded.

"Something that big?" he said. "How could you *not* tell me? I mean, you'd think you'd talk about it all the time–"

"I'm telling you now," Ben said, pointing his spoon. "It wasn't important until now maybe."

"Wasn't important?" Nick asked.

He shook his head. "What was I supposed to do? –One night after soccer take you out on the deck and tell you the story like I did the facts of life?"

"Sure," he said.

"Maybe I screwed up."

Nick sat with both legs beneath him, looking away against the wall–more imagined scenes coursing through his mind. He lifted the saucer closer to his mouth, elbows perched on his knees, and ate thoughtlessly. "Mom know this?" he asked.

"In a kind of outline."

"What do you mean?"

"Doesn't know every detail. I never told her I cried like you did. I never said that exactly. But she knows. She's old enough to color in details." He put the empty dish beside him on the rug. "There's things you don't need to tell people you love," he said. "Maybe they just know because they know you," he said. "You'll understand sometime."

Nick scraped the edges of his bowl and ate what remained, then left the spoon upside down inside in his mouth. "What was her name?" he said.

"Sally–her name was Sally."

"Killed?" he said, "really?"

"You want to know the truth, Nick?" Ben said. "I cried–I swear it–I cried every night for six months maybe. That was long before Mom."

Nick pulled the spoon from his mouth, but kept it in the air in front of his face, then turned toward his father and jabbed, as if some idea had appeared in his head. He raised his finger slowly up off the handle of the spoon as if calling for quiet, thinking some ideas barely discernable in his mind, this single finger like the lit candle of the Sunday School ditty; but it wasn't praise, it was something else. For a moment he sat there, staring at his erect finger and the spoon, as if verifying himself, like babies do, as if his own flesh was a miracle. He turned that hand inward, pointing at the very center of his chest, his whole hand drawn to his heart like a divining rod. "And I'm here—right, Dad?" he said. He looked up at his father. "After this Sally—your girlfriend going down in a plane and all of that crying and a whole year or six months or whatever—I'm still here, right?" "You're very much here," Ben said.

"If this Sally hadn't been killed, there'd be no Mom."

"There'd be no Mom," Ben said.

He pulled at his T-shirt to remind himself it was real. "That says something," he said. "I mean, *I* say something, don't I? — Me. I'm proof. You lost big time, Dad—but you still got me." He had to smile. "I don't mean it that way—"

"I know," he said, and he kissed the top of Nick's head. "You're here, Nick," he said. He put the spoon back in the saucer, and the cat wandered between them, eyeing the empty bowls.

"Sometime, Dad," Nick said slowly, "I want to hear that whole story. I mean, every detail—not now." He seemed to shiver. "But sometime, you know, before this is over, and before Mom comes back. When it's just you and me and the girls in bed like this or something." He raised that finger again, like a preacher. "I want to know who she was—this Sally was. Is that okay?"

Ben nodded.

"You really loved her?" he said again.

Of course, he told himself. "That night," he said, "I didn't see a thing in front of me but some huge black wall all the way to heaven." For the first time in a long time, he thought the father in him had got something right.

"You think I ought to go back to Quinn's?" Nick asked.

Ben tapped the face of his watch. "What does eleven o'clock mean? —Midnight? Time doesn't mean a thing. Nobody's going to sleep." He tipped his head toward the back hall. "Come home anytime–doesn't matter when."

The two of them got up together and took a step into the first hug he'd given his son in far too long, a hug Lynda would have given him a long time ago on this night of death, and a hug that would have made Ben cry had he not held it back because there were already enough tears. "I don't care if you stay overnight," Ben told him. "Quinn needs you just as much as he does his mom and dad right now."

"He was really mad," Nick said. "You should have heard him–"

"People aren't responsible for everything they say at times like this. Keep a big heart, here, okay?" He put his hands on his son's shoulders. "Let stuff go right by."

The two of them walked down the back steps and out the door, down the angling sidewalk toward Nick's car. A bit of a wind jostled the stillness, and streetlights at the corner seemed a blessing, holding back the darkness.

Nick climbed into his car, started the engine, then rolled down the window in order to say one more thing. "He'll be happy to see me," he said. "I know he will. But sometime I want to hear that story." Then he reached for the gearshift. "Can I tell him? – Quinn, I mean," he said. "It's okay if I say about the girl–the one you loved?"

"You tell him what he ought to hear," Ben said.

He nodded and pulled the car into reverse, backed out slowly, the gravel in the alley cracking beneath the tires, then stopped at the street like an old man scrupulously looking both ways, even though there wasn't a soul around.

Upstairs the girls were far into their dreams. Ben walked up the sidewalk to the door, but instead of going upstairs headed for the basement office. In the third drawer of a file cabinet he kept all sorts of things he never looked at. He fanned through the folders until he came to the one he knew held the only letter from a shoe box he'd long ago thrown away, the one letter he couldn't bring himself to destroy.

Church stationary–"Grace Church, Standing Rock, New Mexico." He found it quickly. It was one of those things you don't forget. He opened the envelope and slid out the letter, three pages, both sides, little circles for dots atop the i's.

He read it over quickly. He *was* in love, because love was all there was in that letter, really: how anxious she was to come home, how she'd missed him, how the kids were so good, and how great an experience she was having, how uplifting for her faith, how she missed him so much and wished she could talk to him every night after long, hot days in that little church that wasn't air-conditioned. "It's so quiet at night here in the desert," she wrote. "You wouldn't believe how quiet it gets, how dark. It's beautiful. It really is. Skies full of stars. Actually coyotes. I'm not kidding." Then, finally, "Lots of love, Sally."

And then, what she always wrote, at the end of every letter: "P. S. I miss you tons!!" Two exclamation points.

Even after thirty years, the letter felt like a part of himself; but he tucked the it back in the envelope and wondered if maybe now, after what had happened, he should throw it away–not for Lynda, nor Nick, and not for the little girls, who might never know at all, but maybe for the Lord of earth and heaven, the great magician, who somehow, even in pain brought all things together for good. Something had come full circle, pain become blessing for this single anguished night.

He looked up at the bookshelves, Lynda's lit texts, her novels, a shelf full of his journals, a couple hundred his books full of learning and healing; and on the top shelf beside a golf trophy and a box full of tapes from years ago, a Bible, the little Dutch Bible his father told him he'd toted through the war and read from, night after night, in the middle of all the Nazi treachery. And what did he really know about his father?

He left the drawer open, put the letter on top of the files, and walked to the computer, swung out the desk chair, and hit the switch. He looked at the clock. In South Africa it wasn't yet seven. Lynda might want him to call—she would if she knew what had happened, if she had seen her son cry. But one of the blessings about her going to South Africa was something he knew she'd felt, something he'd brought up himself: by being alone, she could concentrate, not be worried about meal schedules.

She didn't need this sadness, he thought—an accident that killed a girl she'd never known. She could do nothing tonight, after all—nothing but feel guilty about being way over there and not being home. Later, he could write it all.

The computer Nick had picked out was on-line with the Lynda's network at the University. They'd kept it hooked up so they could e-mail each other to their hearts' content. So he logged in and pulled up her address quickly from the file.

"Dear Lynda," he wrote, the letters' magic appearance still fascinating to him. "We just had a kind of crisis. Quinn's girlfriend—her name is Shannon Timmons—was killed tonight. I didn't really know her. There were lots of tears..."

He let the cursor flash and weighed a dozen ways to describe Nick's grief, each of them painful to recount. He typed in a period.

What was there to say? —So much that would hurt her. His fingers curled over the keys like a pianist's. And then he typed, "I think he'll make it." Then deleted "I think"–sounded too tentative, as if there were moments when he worried Nick might not. Then deleted "he'll make it." Tried something else: "He's starting to hold his head up." Let it sit. Tried to imagine how she'd read those words. Deleted "starting to hold," and typed in "holding." Sounded stronger. "He's a good kid," he wrote. Hit *enter*.

What to say? How to describe what happened, without destroying her?

The dehumidifier whirred at the door to the bathroom. Nothing but darkness in the little basement window above the bookshelf, the desk awash with CD-ROMs Nick had a habit of not putting away.

What to say? How to tell her?

"We're working through it," he typed. "Some tears, more than a few, but morning's on the way." He liked that. It was enough. "Hope all goes well," he wrote, then return, and then his initials.

Something's still missing, he thought–something he needed to say.

He brought his fingers back to the keys: "I miss you tons," he wrote, stuck in three exclamation points, looked over what he'd done with a kind of thanks, then spanked the right keys and the message was gone.

What A Man Would Do

His head wasn't in it, and he knew it. Not until he stepped into the circle and pulled himself into a crouch did he realize the wind was gusting from the west, perfect for a record. Any other day he would have felt it first thing in the morning. But the meet was the last thing on his mind.

He pumped three or four more times, carrying the disc behind him, then, in three quick turns in the circle spun every bit of anger and frustration into his hand, his fingers, and the disc, heaved it out and up with a grunt he had to fake. The big wind picked it up, but turned it over way too fast and it dropped dead, ten feet inside the chalk line.

"Good throw," the judge said.

Like hell. He stepped out of the ring from behind and saw his coach leaning up against the fence, showing him thumbs up, a big smile on his face as if the throw were major league. "Don't forget that 200." Coach mouthed, pointing behind at the track.

Darren nodded and turned back. Some kid was poking a metal pin in the ground where his disc had sliced the turf. At best 153, he thought. The difference between big time and playground stuff was having his head together. And his wasn't.

And he knew why. He knew very well why. Saturday night was why. It hadn't been his party and it hadn't been his booze. The whole business of going over to that girl's place wasn't his idea of a good time. He didn't like it the moment the guys he was with decided they were going. Didn't like it because of Kristine being out of town—sure, but his girlfriend wasn't the whole reason it was a bad deal either. There was more to it. The whole idea of some big-time party with some women from some other school—it was trouble, right from the start. But he hadn't said a thing. That was his fault.

"Hensley, Dickinson," the judge yelled, and a tall kid with glasses stepped into the ring.

It was a dual meet, and nobody expected him to lose. He could have taken first place simply by standing at the edge of the circle and grunting out one humungous reverse. That's what he felt like doing—perfect wind or not. Just grunt one out, win this thing, and get the heck out of there.

"Dickinson" it said on the guy's jersey—his mother's school.

And moving—moving out of Shorewood wasn't his idea either, wasn't his fault. It was his mother's idea, picking up the pieces and coming to a town nobody'd ever heard of, just down the road from the school where she'd taken a new job to start all over again. "I don't want to live in a glass house, a single mom in a small town—new and everything," she'd told them. "I don't want to live in the same little town where I teach." She'd looked at him, the oldest. "You don't mind, do you, Darren?" she'd said. "What's the difference? —I'm the one who's got to commute."

What did he know about small towns? The only place he'd ever lived was Shorewood. What could he say? Besides, he'd seen her broken, his own mom coming apart at the seams when his father left her behind like dried-up bait. And he'd been the one to hold her up. He'd held his mother in place himself for more than a couple months or she would have tucked away in some loony bin.

So he and Steph went to Mallard High School and his mother taught at Dickinson, and they were forever away from Shorewood, where he would have been on an ace track team if it hadn't been for his whoring father, who never gave them diddly except for money, really. Plenty of that. "Need this? —Sure." That kind of thing. That was the bottom line with the old man, he told himself. Bastard took some hot-pants accountant or something to the cottage, their cottage, and planked her right there where his own family had spent what people called "quality time." Found himself a brand new sweetie, something with sparkle to haul around on his arm. Burned his mother but bad with a hot time in the old family cottage. Isn't that the American way? And he was doing it for more than a year already when his mother finally caught on to what the old man was doing at the family cottage. *Family cottage*—sure.

The kid from Dickinson let out a throw that got out to maybe 130 feet, but he spun out and flopped in front of the circle. The judge didn't yell "foul" because he didn't need to.

"Van Baron, Dickinson—up," the judge yelled.

Dickinson—his mother's school. Guidance counselor. Divorced woman she was—"tell your problems to somebody who's already seen it all." That's the way he had it figured.

Last night—Monday—she'd cooked up something special. Soup mix over chicken and rice, something with onion in it, and peas, a hot dish, something different he'd recognized right away as either a treat or a guilt trip or something weird. Most of the time she'd come back from school dead tired and stick something frozen in the microwave. Not last night. Hot dish in a casserole. Fancy rolls he and Steph liked—those big, flaky round things. Some kind of special night—he'd recognized it right away, but she didn't say a thing right off. That's what made him think it was guilt. "We don't eat well. Don't eat the right kinds of foods," she'd say sometimes, punishing herself, and then start on a crusade of pot roasts, stuff like that.

You couldn't really tell about her since the old man left. She was different. They all were—he was too, and so was Steph, his sister. The whole world belly-flopped when the old man picked up the bunny and burned them all. His mother was tougher in a way, but sometimes not. More scared probably, sometimes soft as a girl. Maybe that was to be expected. She got her bell rung. She's running down the field, doing her thing, and out of nowhere the old man blindsides her but good. That's the way it seemed, although maybe he didn't know everything either—maybe she'd known a whole lot more than she ever put on before the whole messy business blew up. Maybe she had something figured about the old man—something she smelled. Mother wasn't dumb. And in a way they got closer too, the two of them – him and her. Probably had to, really. All she had left was him and Steph.

Steph was too young to get the whole picture. Last night, his mom had this whole banquet thing cooked up, but Steph didn't know how to read her, didn't figure the fancy catering and the silence was covering something. So the whole time they were eating, Steph kept up this junior high jabber. All during the meal and even after, when they're cleaning up. "Leslie's parents let her go out with Paul," she says. That wasn't news; it was a gripe. "You know? –Leslie Friedley? –The one with the hair, Mom? She can go out on weekends and she's not even thirteen."

What she meant was, why can't I?

"We'll talk about it later," Mom says, opening the dishwasher. "You go practice piano. "We got things to talk about—me and your brother."

"What things?" Steph says.

"Things you don't have to hear."

"That's not fair—"

"*We* got things, too," she'd tells her, "your brother and me. You and I aren't the only ones with personal stuff."

She'd known everything, his mother had—who was at the party, what and how much there was to drink, what time people left—the whole sorry mess. Somebody came into her office, she'd told him, some teary girl, and spilled her guts.

"I want you to know that I know," she says. "But I want you to know this too—I'm breaking every law in the book by talking to you like this. It's unprofessional, but I'm doing it because you're my son," she says. And then, "A girl came to see me—"

Had to be the one called Adrie.

"She told me about this party with Mallard guys. At Sumner's house. She said it was at Angie Sumner's house on Apple River Road—Friday night."

He carried their glasses to the cupboard.

"Don't run away," she says. "I know very well somebody is getting by with it, and it's not right, Darren. It's not right and you know it, because you know what happened."

125

What did he know? – I mean, really. That he shouldn't have been there–sure. That he'd been with this chick he shouldn't have been with, not with Kristine out of town–he knew that too. That some guys had too much to drink – yeah. That things happened – okay, things happened. But if those women didn't want the heat, they shouldn't play with fire. He flipped open the dishwasher and started pulling out dishes.

"You were there," she says. "I'm sure you were. Kris was out of town. You didn't have a date. You were out with the boys, right?

Out with the boys, she says.

Adrie has got to be the one spilling the whole mess. No dream date either. Got hips like a sow. "Guys want a party?" she says when they saw them in the square. What did she expect–church?

"You were there," his mother says again. "What happened?"

He put the glasses in the washer, slipped the plates like a deck of discs into the bottom rack.

"What happened, Darren?" she says again.

"You already know," he told her. "What'd she tell you–this girl?"

"I want your side," she says. "I've breaking confidence just mentioning it."

Who gives a crap about confidence when the three of them are living in Andy's Mayberry Podunk town because everything in their lives fell apart when the old man left? Who gives two bits about some promise to some big party girl animal cruisin' for guys anyway? Who gives a shit?

"This girl came to me," she says, "because she didn't have anybody else—couldn't tell her parents—you know how people are around here, how strict." He can feel the way she's talking at his back, and she's mad. "This girl doesn't want anybody to know what happened—because of the beer, Darren." And then she says, "Dammit, look at me. Come back into this room and sit down. I mean it."

He could have told her back off, but he would have killed her. He could have sworn at her, but he would have broken her back. She was double-barrel mad. But he hadn't done anything except cheat on Kristine, and that wasn't the big deal because it wasn't anything to speak of. That wasn't what his mother was after either.

"She got *raped*, Darren—this girl," his mother says. "I don't care what the guy says—how you excuse it, who did it, how it happened, what she was wearing—this girl got raped and she can't tell a soul—for reasons that are dead wrong, I think, but they're hers."

She hadn't been that mad since the old man left.

"Nobody's supposed to know about this party, about the drinking." She tosses her head back as if it's plain nuts, and it is. "She gets raped, and nobody's supposed to know about beer, and I'm the guidance counselor and I've got to play along, see? –Even though I want somebody to hang." She's got fists. "She got raped, dammit, and somebody got away with it–some cocky high school kid, some–"

"*Guy*," he says. "Just say *male*, Mom–that's what you want to say, don't you?"

"Okay, some *guy*," she says. "Some guy who thinks he's a man because he put a notch in his gun–whatever it is men do."

"Geez –" he says.

"Well, it's true." She points at him. "Who's bragging, Darren? –That's what I want to know. Who's the loud mouth? You know." She's got that finger raised. "Who came out of that party bragging. You've had to have heard." And then, eyes full of blitz. "It wasn't you? –God Almighty, I pray it wasn't you–"

"It wasn't me," he says.

She wipes her fingers through her eyes.

"How do you know you got the whole truth?" he says.

"I do," she says.

"Because we're all alike–is that it? You can't trust any of us? Because that's the way we are–every last guy on the planet? We're all bad asses, right?"

"I know when people are telling the truth," she says.

"Maybe I'm telling the truth," he says. "Maybe she's lying – this girl. You ever think of that? There wasn't any Barbie dolls at that party, Mom—""

"No Kristines either," she says.

Blackmail.

"You know, don't you?" she says. And then, right away, "She got raped, Darren. That's the truth. Some things you just know." She took his hand. "I want to know who," she said. "I can't do a thing legally, but I want to know–and I want you to know. You're my son. I raised you better than this."

What he wanted to say was something about the old man, but he couldn't–not just then. He could have too–he could have brought it up, how he was raised. He could have thrown it in her face. Outside the patio door the lawn is starting to green. It's a late spring, and a squirrel is hanging upside down from the clothesline pole, trying to get to the bird feeder like they always do.

"So who were you with?" she says. "Kristine is gone for the weekend. There's a bunch of girls from another school, plenty of beer. Which one of my students were you with, Darren?"

"Nobody," he says. A lie.

"I know better," she says. "Kids tell me things. I'm the counselor, remember?"

"Does everybody know everybody here?" he says.

But he can't help but remember. The bedroom in that party house belonged to some little girl. There's a picture of great-

great grandparents, a man in a chair and his fat wife behind him, something out of the Gold Rush or something–that old, like saints on the wall. A dresser with two Japanese boxes full of earrings and bracelets–girl stuff, like Steph's. A Bible on the little table beside the bed. Kid's Bible–white cover, with pictures, one of those. And there he was. Kristine was gone. Some girl it wasn't dark enough not to see in the light of one of those huge farm lights making the whole place bright as day through the window, even though the shade was drawn. Whatever he'd do, she'd giggle. Lois, she said, something like that. Dumb name – Mayberry name if he ever heard one. Two open beers parked beside a frilly photo albums on the table with a Daffy Duck light. And there's some giggle-box beside him.

"It wasn't me," he told his mother, because it wasn't him either. He wasn't lying. Not that he wouldn't have gone the whole nine yards right then and there. But he didn't force anything. The whole room smelled like his little sister. And more. His old man was in there, too. His old man was in him, in his molecules, in his genes. He's lying there beside this giggling girl and he gets this big bad look into the darkness inside him, and what he finds is his own old man. "I didn't rape anybody, Mom," he tells her, because he didn't.

"I believe you," she says. "But you know who did." She's grabs a hold of his hand. "And I want to know."

"Why?" he says.

"Because I don't want the guy ever again in my house."

That's what happened.

He snaps back. He's at the meet. It's a dual, and he's got one lousy throw out there, and the judge yells his name. "Nikkles, Mallard—on deck," he said. It's Tuesday, right? But the whole business isn't over by a long shot. He's got two more throws and he's got to go face his mother again.

And the fact is he knows who did what she said. If somebody raped a girl that night, he knows very well who it was.

He steps back into the ring, winds up his arm, and pulls himself into the crouch. He stops for a minute and looks over towards the fence. Coach is already back across the track now that the far stake belongs to a Mallard kid.

He glances over to the shot circle, where he sees Ben Warren holding the shot-put high above his head while he stretching his hamstrings. "When I went in that bitch, I could have been driving a truck," he'd said that night. "She was eating out of my hand." And then he turned to him, looked over the front seat, and he says, "What'd you get, Nikkles?" – as if it was the day after Christmas and they were comparing gifts. Ben Warren leans up from the back seat, flicking the pop-top of a Miller Draft. "What'd you get, big-city boy?" he says again, as if it was a contest.

Two more throws. His arm was loose. He waited for the wind to rise—then, once it did, he went into his spin, stayed low and exploded. The disc took off into a gust, perfect plane, going up and up and then flipping over and carrying out way past the chalk line.

"Foul," the judge said.

His toe was over the line. The kid never put in a stake because she heard the judge yell.

"Too bad, Nikkles," the judge said, the band director. "That was a whopper."

He walked out the circle and spotted Kristine coming over to the circle, wearing his old Shorewood jacket, and trying to keep her hair out of her eyes in the wind.

"What you tell Kristine is your problem," his mother had said last night. "Don't ask for any sympathy from me, but you better tell her."

It was stupid and bad and wrong and he felt like shit after he'd left this party. *Party*. You want to call it a *party*? Country boys idea of fun–get polluted and get women.

He turned around and pulled his sweatshirt over his shoulders and his arm, pretended he didn't see Kristine, his eyes on the guy from Dickinson in the ring.

"That must be yours way out there," she said when he felt the points of her fingers in the back of his ribs, a little hug from her arms. "*Way* out there?" she said. "So what's up? –How many left?"

"One," he told her, not looking back.

"Coach said I shouldn't come over because everything was right today and you were going into outer space—that's exactly what he said." She dropped the little hug and came around beside him. "'Don't distract him,'—those are his very words."

She didn't know, and maybe she wouldn't have to.

"Got a B in chemistry, Darren," she told him. "I could have lit a match and blown the place up."

"Got a B?" he mimicked.

"Really stupid test," she said. "So you want me to stay or not? —Last throw, right? You need to concentrate?"

"Last throw," he said.

Lois whatever, the giggle-box. Not *in* bed with her, just on it. Little small-town girl all goosey over the big-city boy. "I always dreamed of going to high school in Milwaukee," she said. Lois or Leah or whatever. He's lying there in a bedroom like Steph's and he thinks of the cottage and his old man.

"Want me to leave?" Kristine said.

"Stay," he told her.

The night it all broke loose between his parents, his mother bawled and screamed and swore and he was the one with his arms around her, the man of the house all of a sudden. Both of them hated the old man that night—the man he still couldn't call his father, wouldn't ever call his father, not any more.

When he climbed into the ring, he saw his old man's face over the field like a huge sand bag target, a face with a gaping mouth cut out of wood. What you remember is Brewers games, chipping golf balls, and the time he came home with a new set of weights; what you remember is the cottage, the smell of the lake, the sand—hot on your feet and gritty in your food. What you remember is the times when everything is the way it ought to be and good like that. You don't even imagine what crap can happen, not really—when you're a kid. Who could imagine? Who'd want to? Who'd care to know what kind of shit happens?

He spun, harder and faster, staying low, and when he exploded out of the crouch, he stuck that throw. He pushed every last ounce of strength and weight into the end of his finger, winged the disc up into that great wind, and he got it. He got the big one. The monster. He got the throw off he wanted to all year long. It kept on going and kept on going. He got it up there almost forever. Nobody spoke. Nobody said a thing. It was that kind of heave. He got the gold and all of that shit. He got the school record. It sailed over the kid's head, out there beyond the chalk, lifted a puff a dust when it came down in the next county.

"Huge," the judge said. "You got that one up there, Nikkles."

And he did. Big deal.

Kristine hugged him when he stepped out of the circle—when he stepped out of the circle, she actually came up and hugged him. Her arms felt like pain.

"I got to run," he told her, pulling away fast. "I got a relay." He didn't even wait for a distance. It was out there past 160'.

Ben Warren says not to outrun him on the hand-off of the relay. Ben Warren says he never has much juice left when he's finished 'cause he's a stupid runner, going flat out the way he does and Darren shouldn't outrun him because he's likely to fall flat on his face when he finishes. Ben Warren says he starts out like gangbusters and forgets he's got to pace himself. It's all I know how to do, he says. Ben Warren says not to make him look like a fool. There's people in the stands. Women.

The four of them prance around in the middle of the field, practicing hand-offs. Ben Warren says he doesn't want to drop the baton because there's a college coach in the bleachers, and it's not track he's gives two hoots about anyway, but football. The guy's from Stevens Point, he says, and he wants him to play football. He doesn't want to look like a turkey and mess up the whole relay, even though the race doesn't mean shit. That's what Ben Warren says.

"Just don't outrun me," he says. "And remember you don't have to look back, because I'll blast you with the baton. You'll feel it. I like to ram it home, you know," and then he laughs.

Those are the words he remembers when the gun sounds and Blake takes off in the lead, like always—when he watches him round the track, body low to the ground, arms pumping, that baton up there eye level when his hand reaches. What Ben says is in his mind when he sees the first hand-off, smooth as silk, and watches Ben Warren hold the lead, even gain for a while—ten yards in front of the guy from Dickinson. What he's thinking is how Ben likes to ram it home.

And it's just like he told him—when he's coming up the stretch, Ben's juice is gone. So he doesn't take off too fast. He turns around to watch him coming, holding his body up too high the way Ben always runs, the baton out front in the wrong hand, and all the time he tells himself he hates this guy's absolute guts. The whole party was his idea, chicks from some other school—who cares anyway? And then he feels that baton slam into his hand, and he knows very well who it was. He knows it was Ben Warren.

His legs flow. His feet eat up the track, and he knows, too, that he has never run faster. He feels like the wind. He's riding on something on high, like the disc, and the whole time he's running, he feels as if he's leaving earth behind. It's all back there because he's leaving it, running, flying. He keeps reaching, his lungs big as the sky, and he's not fighting a thing as his legs come up beneath him like featherlites, the track disappearing. He feels like he wants to keep running right into eternity, right off the track and out of town to some new place—not Shorewood either, not Mallard, just keep running and put all way behind. He could run for miles, all the way to the Chicago, all the way to Atlanta.

Wilkerson breaks out ahead of him, and he knows that all he's got to do is deliver it, and he does, perfectly, in a way that makes him to go his knees when he's finished, not because he's tired—because he's not, but because he's got to cry, dammit – he's somehow got to cry. He's stoops right there, all the way across the track from the crowd in the bleachers, holds his jersey on his knees to hide the tears even though he doesn't even know the reason why.

When he looks up he sees Ben Warren and Wilkerson doing this big dance right in front of the crowd. High fives. Blake is already over there. Victory dance for a two-bit dual meet in some Podunk town where they were going to build a new life. But he stays down as if he's beat, nauseous or something. Coach is there in the middle of it. And then they all come to the middle of the field, for him. The first slap from Blake makes him wince.

"Good night," Coach says to him, "and *into* the wind. I'm going to put you in more often. What a split."

"Hey, city boy," Ben says, and he comes at him, both hands raised.

He doesn't raise his hands, doesn't want to prance, doesn't want to make it this big thing, doesn't want to touch anybody. So Ben picks him up in a bear hug and lifts him off the ground. He wants to cuss and scream, but he can't. He can't, and he can't be stupid either. He can't be a jerk now, can't be someone who doesn't make a big deal so he does the thing he doesn't want to do, does the thing he hates himself for—he lifts his hands like this is Olympics. He lifts his hands in triumph so he doesn't look like a girl or something. He's in Ben Warren's arms and he acts like this stupid race is the really biggest deal of all.

He avoids Kristine when he leaves. He comes off the track at the far side, close to the road, swings the fence shut behind him, hurrying to get back and get showered. And that is when he sees his mom standing beside her car.

"I don't know how you can do it," she says, because she knows every last thing. She knows it's Ben Warren. "I don't understand how my son can do what you did, knowing everything." *Everything*, she says, meaning not just the party. She's got her arms up over her chest, and she's leaning against the door of the car. "If anybody knows what's right, you should—after what we've been through, Darren."

She's crying. He's seen it before, too often this last year. She's bawling. And then she leaves. She doesn't say another word. She leaves him.

*

He was still in his sweats when he got close to the cottage. It was almost two hours north, and he was proud of himself for what he'd done—leaving without going home, just driving up the lake shore alone. It was dark, but he knew the roads without looking, felt the highway narrow the closer he came to the cottage, traffic falling away because it was a Tuesday night in late spring, there was no traffic north of the city, and it's still cold on the lake shore.

What his father told him that night they talked for the first time, for the only time, was that someday he'd understand what his father had done. "You're almost a man," he'd said. "Someday you'll understand because you'll know, too. You can almost grow a beard," he'd said, laughing. Laughing. The guy's laughing. "It never was right, Darren," he told him. "What you have to understand is that it never was right between your mother and me, and you can't live with what you don't love. You'll know. You're almost a man. You'll understand. I don't expect you to forgive me now, but some day you will. I'd bet on it."

In the old days, they'd stayed up late after long days on the beach, feeling that glow you get from all day in the sun. They'd play Rook and Old Maid and Chinese Checkers in the light of a lamp or two and the fire, snapping and crackling, a fire you could gaze at for hours with the sound of the waves outside rocking the whole place into sleepiness. Looking into a fire, hearing the water. Things like that put you to sleep almost—staring into a fire, listening to the surf quiet down for the night. Something good, something forever.

Right there at that cottage, his father laid the secretary. For months it went on, and now he was going to burn it down, he told himself. It didn't just come to him either. He'd thought about it for a long time. When he got to the lane, he parked the car up at Rasmussen's. No one was around. It was cold on the lake.

He hiked up the beach past the Andersons, the Burrell's, the Angoras–past the old bleached stump shining like a ghost in the moon just coming up over the waves, cold as silver ice. He jogged in the cold, hard sand along the shore until he came to the cove, and then came to the place where the cottage stood beneath the pines, this little cottage, Grandpa's cottage, nothing spectacular either, an antique just over the dune at the edge of the woods. It was no palace, but they'd had good times there. No kidding. If it were lighter out ne'd have been able to see the peak he'd painted himself not that long ago, leaning down from a perch on the roof.

He walked to the door and tried it, but it was locked; so he went around back, picked up the big pail at the back porch, and when he got to the bathroom window put the it down to get up high enough to reach above the sill for the key. It wasn't there.

Had to be his father that took it. Had to be. They always kept it there.

Ever since he left the track, he'd been thinking that he had to do it. The place had to be torched. There had to be an end to something. Couldn't be anything new before something old burned down.

He checked the sill again, but found nothing. He had no matches. He could knock out a window, get inside, and rip the place apart. For sure he'd get away with it because it happened all the time on the lake, kids trashing cottages. Nobody would know except his parents—and they would know. Make no mistake about that. They'd know. But trashing it wasn't the point. The place had to go.

He pushed the pail under another window and felt along the wet sill, thinking maybe his old man hid the key. Nothing. He stepped down and kicked the pail. It tumbled down the hill and into the trees. He walked around the side porch, past windows drawn and curtained. The moon lit the place brightly, the birches still leafless and white as dry bones.

He felt through the cut wood piled at the side of the house, found a log small enough to wield, something he could get in his hands, then looked around. Nothing moved anywhere. Nobody was down at the lake shore this time of year. He was the only one around.

He'd married her, that accountant or secretary or whatever, the woman he brought up here.

He rolled the chunk of branch in his hands as he stepped up on the porch, and took a swing at the porch light. Glass shattered and fell over the floor.

Your old man drinks, and you do. Your old man beats your old lady, and you do. Isn't it that the way it works? Your old man lies and you do. You are sure enough what your old man is.

He backhanded the window to his parents' bedroom, the glass splashing inside. With the end of the log, he spattered out the jagged pieces from the frame, pulled the curtain aside, climbed up on the metal chair just outside, as if to pull himself through, then looked at the bed. When he and Steph were asleep on the bunks upstairs, his parents slept there—before the princess accountant or whatever. His step-mom. Whoever wants a step-mom? Who asks for one? All he could see now was this other women, his father's bulk over her in this bed, their bed, destroying absolutely everything with a hot time in the old cottage, getting his jollies.

There's matches on the mantle, he thought. He pushed his legs through the open window then leaned back to pull his upper body through. Dark inside, but he didn't need light to know his way around. He moved through the bedroom, felt the rug quit before he came to the apron of stone in front of the grate. The kerosene lamp. He held it in his hands, saw the shade. Things got clearer.

Two boxes of matches stood beside a kachina doll his father had taken back from New Mexico. Round, flat stones from the beach lined up in a row that he'd put them there himself when he was a kid, ones he'd picked up on the beach, jammed in his pockets. Magazines down below—kindling.

He put down the log, slipped open the box, and picked out maybe ten wooden matches, lit one quickly and looked around. He had every good reason in the world to burn it down, every last excuse rising from something in his heart—no, not in his heart. It wasn't his heart. It was something in him spilling hate and already burning so hot he didn't need matches. All he had to do was to touch his finger to a grocery bag and the place would go. Hate was what it was. Hate in him.

He stood there, lit another match when the first went out, turned and looked around the place—the chairs, the couch, the games beneath the corner table. Not out of anger, he told himself. He couldn't do this because he was pissed. That was wrong. Something just had to go, he thought. Something had to die. Something had to burn. There had to be an end to something. There was something right about it—the cottage goes up in flames and they know who did it. It was like telling him something he couldn't say. The place is burned down and they look at him and they can't say a thing because they know too well why. They can't even yell. Nobody can. His old man can't—and his mother either—because then they'd very damn well know what they'd done. More than he could say. Better than he could ever tell them with words.

He balled up some newspapers and dropped them on the throw rug, then picked the kerosene lamp up and smashed it over the floor, lit another match, and waited. In his hand, the flame of the match broke into pieces on the shaft. Ben Warren would do it, he told himself, turning the match in his fingers to keep it lit. Ben Warren was a man. Ben Warren wouldn't hesitate here for a minute. Ben Warren would do it and smile. Ben Warren would be proud of himself. Let it go, let it drop. Ben Warren would just laugh. Ben Warren would make it a big deal—high fives all around.

A man would just do it, he thought. A man would burn the place down and laugh. Like his old man. Just laugh. What a man would do. Something's his old man would do, sure thing.

The night sky was clear when he walked back towards the lake and sat, still in his sweats, alone on the crown of the beach, the moon still scattering sparkles over the rough hide of the water, the sky dark as velvet spread with stars, the cottage–the love nest, their cottage, Grandpa's cottage–completely hidden in darkness, but still there, still standing. No flames. Quiet and still. With the edge of his hood, he dried his eyes.

Behind him, the sound of waves lapping. Like rain at night. You can listen to that all night long, he thought–just listen to a mystery. Like looking into a fire. You can sit and stare forever.

He took a wooden match out of the pouch of his sweatshirt and lit it with his fingernail. You can sit and stare for hours. He pulled the match up in front of his face, flicked his wrist and twisted it out, then looked at the lake, so gentle it seemed untouched, a field of soft gray darkness no single disc had ever cut. And beyond and over it, a sky and a hundred million stars in galaxies so far outside of anywhere that nobody had ever dreamed they existed. Black holes big enough to swallow continents. So much out there, so very much.

There's things that are bigger, he thought.

There's got to be.

First Bride

By Dutch standards, the house is not old–at best, at very best, one hundred years. Fortress-like, red brick, hip-roofed in long, thick thatch, it stands 200 meters back from a country lane meandering up and out from the Veluwe, a woody area of the Netherlands we might call a national forest. The area is very provincial; most Dutch people would call it backward. I once met a man from Ermelo who told me people consider the whole region twenty years behind the times; he jerked the visor of his cap, hurrumphed a bit, and told me he wished it were 25.

Nothing about the house distinguishes it. Surrounded by a few trees and a wooden fence covered with something like chicken wire, the place is quintessentially Dutch, from its steep roofs to the small barn that is not out back of the house, but is the house's own spacious back room. A few trees line its brick lane, and unused wooden lawn furniture sits in a square patch of yard created where the front wall of what used to be the barn suddenly juts out from the line of the house and looks over that corner with the eye of a new and broad picture window.

On that trip to the Netherlands, my third, I took a small tape recorder, and as I traveled I told it things I didn't want to forget. Not until I stopped the car behind the house did I remember that although that recorder was in my hand and running, I'd been saying nothing.

Exactly what I wanted to tell this woman I didn't know. I didn't resent her; I had no reason to, never having met her, never having even known of her until the day before I pulled up at her back door. If I hadn't stumbled on her name beside my father's on his emigration records, I would have never known she existed. The thought of simply turning around never crossed my mind. Nervous, yes—but as I remember that moment, I was not reluctant, perhaps because I wondered whether the two of us had known completely different men. I wanted her to acquaint me with the father I'd never met.

It was late spring, and the sun had appeared for what seemed to have been the first time since I'd come to the Netherlands four days before. Out back, in the grass north of the house, sheets and pillowcases lay spread over the ground. Even though I'd never seen that done before, I knew—how? By DNA? – that the bedding was being whitened in the old way, bleached by the sun. It was not a kind of deja vu—I felt no flashing echoes. But the thought of my father, years before, standing there himself, out back of this house, at the same exact place, at a time in his life when he was head-over-heels in love, was overwhelming. The war was over. A young woman who lived there would be his bride. I wondered how often he stood right there kissing her passionately. How often, just a few minutes later, did he walk down the lane from this back door, dreaming of the full course of this woman's love, a woman not my mother?

He never once spoke of a first marriage, never hinted at this huge story in his life. Nothing in his demeanor or his frequent sermons to me had ever suggested he'd suffered–the war, yes; I'd heard dozens of stories about the war. But nothing about a first bride. I had no idea there'd been anyone other than my mother. I would never have dared guess, really–and I'm a historian. My father is not secretive or reclusive; with no hesitation, I'd describe him as joyful and jovial. Even on the most forsakenly frigid South Dakota mornings, with the wind tugging at our barn's every shingle and slat, the milking parlor could be as warm as the house, filled as it was with cows, gospel music from the Motorola, and my father's lilting tenor. He was not secretive, not brooding, not dark or silenced. I would have never guessed he could hold the secret of a first marriage so firmly.

But there had been a first wife. Why didn't he tell me? Was it out of some deference to my mother? Or was the whole story that painful–even half a century after it ended? What had he done?

Was it my father's sin, or was it simply my father's pain? Either way, how and why could he cover it so completely?

I make my living on the past. I trade on details. I unearth secrets wherever and whenever I can, trying to make sense of time and place long past. History is my method of putting together a puzzle from pieces scattered hither and yon in a quantity never quite sufficient to complete the whole. But the truth is that I felt somewhat sordid as I stood there behind that Dutch house, digging through my father's past. Back home, he was dying of cancer, and here I was scooping a story for some trashy family tabloid my brothers and sisters would likely be the only ones to read. Who else would care? No one. What difference did it make that he'd married before my mother? But I am a historian. Berendina Janssens, a woman I'd never met, was his first wife. I had to know.

I was in the Netherlands for a conference on Dutch-American immigration, where I had been riffling through data on display–someone's research project newly computerized–when I punched in my father's name, simply to see how the program worked. From the time I was a child I knew the month and year he'd left Holland, where he'd come from, and where and when he'd arrived in Canada. As a boy, I visited the Ontario farm where he worked his first six months. Ten years ago, I met the old man who'd sponsored him, a man who, like my father, had never said a word about a first marriage, even though we'd talked for an hour or more. Had there been a conspiracy? And did my mother know?

Maybe she didn't. Maybe that's why my father never spoke of Berendina Janssens.

During a break between conference sessions, on a whim I typed in my father's name on that computer; the CD-ROM light glowed, and the screen kicked out the whole bill of goods: the date he'd left, the name of the ship that had carried him to Canada, and the name—Berendina Jannsens-Versteeg. My first impulse was to hide the screen from people milling around me. I stooped over the screen as if I'd forgotten my glasses, read the name again and again.

I had only a day to find out something about this woman, so I left the conference that afternoon and drove out to the Veluwe.

The house has a front door, but I don't remember it. All the comings and goings happen by way of the back, where the driveway leads. Behind the house—behind what once was the barn—stands a real barn, small by North American standards, but obviously still something of a dairy. Spread out in back of the place were a few acres of fenced pasture with Jerseys, a picture that could have passed for a Wisconsin tourist poster. It was a bright, clear Saturday morning, not warm but beautiful, the air, like so much of rural Holland, redolent with manure.

The door was barely bigger than a closet door and painted in no distinguishing way. There was a doorbell. I pushed it, quickly, as I remember, because the time that had passed since I'd come up the drive couldn't have been long and I already felt like a trespasser.

A woman stood in shrouded darkness before me almost immediately—small, far too small for my father, who always stooped in the basement of our farm home.

At that moment, I believe I had to fight not to show my nervousness. I deliberately used English. "Berendina Janssens," I said, "is that right?"

She nodded. She seemed younger than my father, significantly younger, a wisp of a woman. That's what I thought. "My name is Gerald Versteeg," I said. "I'm from the U.S. I was at this conference in Utrecht—"

"You may come in," she said, unlatched the door, and stepped aside, looking away with deference not uncharacteristic of older Dutch women.

Something between them had broken, humpty-dumptied forever. He left her—or she him. I was born in '49, and I am, very much, by physical resemblance, my mother's child. That left only two years for my father to start all over again after whatever it was that broke up the brand new marriage he'd come to Canada with. Maybe she was the real reason he'd left for the States.

"My brother me warned me you were coming," she said, her English hardly broken. "He called."

I should have said that my even being there was something of a miracle. I'd met her brother at the Vrijgemaakte church in Heerde, the place to which I'd been directed by a woman at the travelers' center. She'd said there were many Janssens still in town, but two of them of my father's generation would be at her church, working. I lied to that woman; in my halting Dutch I told her I was looking for my mother's family, assuming like the small-towner I am that, even fifty years later and the Nazis long gone, the real story might still be a scandal.

Berendina Janssens' brother was one of a dozen retirees dressed in traditional garb and standing around a little museum and store just behind the church, a place run for the cause of missions in Zaire. I couldn't lie to this man, and once he had squared away who I was, he told me the most astounding news—that this woman who'd been married to my father had, years ago, returned to the Netherlands alone and presently lived here, just outside of town, in the family house. Not for a moment did he hesitate. "You must, of course, see her," he told me, reaching for a pencil from the pocket of his collarless shirt. "It is not a far distance from here, and she is at home." He must have called her just after I left.

"I'm sorry for walking in on you like this—I mean, out of nowhere," I told her as she closed the outside door behind us.

"Don't be," she said. "So many years ago it was that I hardly remember your father so good."

It was dark in the old barn. I couldn't make out her face clearly, but she pointed me toward the back door of the home. I'd heard enough stories about attached barns to fill the place with incidents from the war—men hiding from the Nazis, at least a dozen earthy stories about people relieving themselves back there and getting caught off guard.

"My Dutch isn't as good as it should be," I told her as we walked over the freshly swept cement. "I'm glad you speak English well."

"I lived for ten years in Canada," she said. "But I knew English already before I left–before we did."

"*We*," I said, "meaning my father?"

"Of course," she said. I followed her silhouette through the semi-darkness, the only light coming through that picture window on the far end of the room. She wasn't at all what I had imagined–heavy and square-built, no *dikke vrouw*. She wasn't thick shouldered, wasn't dressed in a smock. She wore slacks, and she wore them so well that my father's interest in her, fifty years ago, was obvious–she would have been a looker.

"So," she said, as we came into the kitchen, "who are you?"

"I thought you knew," I told her. "You said your brother called–"

"I mean, who are you?" Typical Dutch aggression. She didn't turn as she spoke, simply marched me into the kitchen, pulled a chair out from the table for me, then walked to the counter for coffee. "What kind of son might I have had if I stayed with your father?"

"I can't get over your English," I told her. "Do you use it often?"

"In Holland many people speak English—but not of my generation," she said. Two black cups, thick porcelain, she swiped from a tree of cups at the far end of the table, set them down before us, and filled them. "We're not fascists, like the French," she said. "And there is that, of course—" she pointed at the television at the far end of the table.

Berendina Janssens's hair was stylishly short, parted at the side, and cut straight, a wave in her bangs. The lines around her mouth and eyes wouldn't allow falsehood about age, and her fingers, as she poured the coffee, seemed craggy and probably rheumatoid. But when she leaned back from the table and drew her hair away from her face, she made it difficult for me think of her as an old woman. Something undefeated flashed in her eyes, something which a half century ago might well have made my father the hymn singer consider the deep reaches of his desire downright sinful.

She took a chair, sat back with her cup in her hand, twisted herself out from the table slightly, just far enough to cross her legs before her, holding her chin so high as to be defiant. "What do you do?" she said, and then tucked her left arm beneath the one with steaming coffee and looked straight into my eyes. "What brings you to Holland?"

"I'm a professor," I said.

She nodded, as if that passed muster.

In the States, I would have told her I taught in college. "I teach history," I told her. "I'm an Americanist. I teach American history actually."

She nodded again.

I honestly believe that inside me, my father's own genes reached for her. She was that attractive. The way she addressed me was forthright, fully engaged, direct and alive. Those first five minutes she never moved from her chair, but her energy filled the room. Had she been my mother, my life would have been different—I knew it almost immediately.

"Historians," she said, smiling, "are keepers of the facts." She advanced her cup as if it were a weapon. "What *you* people know is the truth."

"Can anyone claim that, really?" I said.

She snuck a peek at my face and winked. "If you think that way, then you must have left your father's church behind," she said. "There, everyone knows all of the truth."

Quick mind. Engaged cynic. "You find my leaving that church a good thing?" I asked.

She shrugged her shoulders. "Are you happy?" she said.

Typically Dutch. Cut-to-the-chase questions.

"Is anyone?" I said.

"Some fortunate few, I think," she said. And then, "What must I call you, 'Professor Versteeg? –"

"Tony," I said.

Under her breath she repeated my name, and then, in Dutch, "Anton," she corrected. "We were saying, some people are happy—and you are one of them?"

"More than some," I said, "less than others."

"And smarter than some, too," she said, quickly. Another wink.

She wore a navy sweater, cotton, crew neck, very traditionally cut, no blouse peeking out at the collar. There were no rings on her hands, nothing to make clear whether or not she had married again. The way she looked at me—when she wasn't speaking, when she wasn't probing—was maternal at times, her eyes measuring in a way I would have found uncomfortable if she were not the woman who'd once married my father. She was doing research, I suppose, using her own methods.

"I am your first husband's son," I said. "What would you like to know?"

She adjusted her glasses with the back of her hand, then took a deep breath, the first sign I read of any reluctance at all. "What did your father tell you?"

At that moment, for a reason I don't know myself, I wanted to protect him. I didn't want her to know that she was a personal secret he'd either hoarded or hated or both. "What must I call you?" I asked.

"Dena," she said, a familiarity I wouldn't have expected.

"And your last name?"

"Janssens," she said, "my family name."

Maybe it was myself I wanted to protect, the historian who'd, ironically, known nothing about his own family record. "Was the marriage annulled?" I asked.

"What did he tell you?" she said again.

I brought the cup up to my lips and took a sip of the strong coffee, then lied. "That it ended," I said.

"That's all?"

My imagination created a conversation in which my father told all. We're in our barn, the milking done, and we're standing alongside the stanchions. He would have told me with a moral imperative, in the same way he told me almost everything. I can see him pointing his finger. And then I told Mrs. Janssens, "He told me it didn't matter what happened. What he'd learned was that you have to pick up the pieces and go on." I hunched my shoulders quickly, as he might have. "'Bad things happen,' he said, 'but the point is not to let them ruin your life.'" And then I smiled my father's consecrated smile. ""Suffering can make you strong'—that's what he said. 'The thing is to grow from adversity.'" I was sounding like Robert Schuller.

At that point, I'm not sure she even heard what I'd said. She held up a hand, uncrossed her legs, put her cup on the table, and pointed to what may have been a trapdoor in the floor. "That's where he was, you know—that's where he stayed," she said. "For six months, the man lived with us—six months. I was seventeen and every able-bodied man around was off somewhere, hiding or gone."

"My father?" I said.

"I didn't even know your father then," she said. "Oh, maybe by family—maybe I could picture him—his walk, his thick hair, that high wave. I knew *of* him, you might say, but I didn't know him."

I had no idea who she was talking about, but I did understand that even though I had been in Dena Janssens' house for no more than five minutes, she'd already cut to very heart of a story I hadn't heard in all of my years with my father.

"He lived here with us for almost six months at the very end of the war, and I loved him," she told me, her clenched lips enforcing the passion she remembered. "My mother would have killed me—she was one of you people."

I suspected what she meant by that was something religious, but I let her speak.

"It was dangerous really, for my parents to let them talk with us—with the children." She pointed again. then kicked back the rug. "Look, look at your feet."

There beneath me was enough of square line to recognize that just below the kitchen table had been the hiding place, a cellar for whoever it was the Janssen family hid from the Nazis—*onderduikers*, maybe Jews.

"It was frightfully stupid," she said. "I didn't know that then, but I've thought of it often since that time. It was one thing," she told me, "for my parents to hide them here, but it was another altogether for them to let us mingle with them—and the younger children." She swept both hands up in a gesture of silliness. "Who knows? One of my sisters may have picked up an English word or phrase and used it at church in front of someone who should not have known we were hiding Canadian pilots."

And that's when I knew the story. She'd fallen in love with a Canadian. She'd been in love with a Canadian pilot—but then why didn't she emigrate herself—a war bride? She must have used my father as a means to immigrate, then left him.

"My mother would have killed me if she knew. My father would have thrown me out of the house." She looked around her, at the stove and the laundry tree across the room, the tiles on the walls. "This house," she said, chuckling, "the one I live in now. He would have thrown me out, to be sure—a sinner because there was a baby—his baby. I needed your father."

As a pretext for getting to Canada, she'd married my father, used him as a means of finding the pilot her family had harbored and she'd loved. She was very young; and in the middle of all that war mess, she'd fallen head over heels. This woman. She was pregnant.

"I'm like a rabbit, I suppose," she said. "Isn't it a rabbit that's supposed to move in circles—that's supposed to always return to its *hokken*? Now, here I am."

"A rabbit," I said, "yes. And me too, I suppose. Because here we sit—you and me."

"This is not your home," she said coldly. "You're not coming back to anything. You have no blood here."

I retaliated in kind. "How can you say that? My father's blood is on the back step," I told her. "I felt it when I stood there before coming in." She must have lied to him, told him he was the father—and it had to be fast, everything had to be fast. She had to have taken my father very, very quickly, then used his righteousness. "And his love is spilled here somewhere too, isn't it?" I said. "It haunts the place—it must be here—"

"Not his," she said. "My Canadian hero's is here," she said bitterly, "but not your father's. I don't hate him. I never did." There was no pretense in her, no politics but truth, but sometimes it seemed as if when she looked at me, she saw a lower species. "You love your father," she said. "And you should. But I didn't—never."

"I lied," I told her. "My father never mentioned your existence—not once in his life. I never knew of a first bride."

Her eyes turned to steel, and the corners of her lips fell.

"Until yesterday, Mrs. Janssen, I didn't even know you existed," I told her. "I had absolutely no idea my father married you. I knew nothing about his taking a wife to Canada." Each line hit her hard, so I kept at it, assaulting her for reasons I really didn't know fully. "You can't imagine how surprised I was when I found your name with his," I told her. "My father married! He never spoke of you—not a word. Never mentioned you. Only by accident am I here—only by luck. You understand?"

She reached for her cup, gathered what she could of her strength before lifting her eyes to mine once again. And then, some dignity coming back, she said, "So what do you expect me to believe," she said, "this first story or now the second one?"

I pulled the chair up close to the table. "Look at me," I said. "I'm telling you that not once in my father's life did he mention a word about you. I didn't know you existed until—" I looked at my watch, "until yesterday. Not even 24 hours ago."

She looked across the room, pulled her arms back from the table, sat straight on her chair, then lifted herself quickly and stepped back. "That's why I left him," she said. "Damned Christians and their stoic nonsense—if you don't talk about it, it doesn't exist." She raised her hands to her waist, stood there straight and proud. "Damn them—damn them all for their secret sins. Damn them all for their righteousness and their Godliness. Isn't that like them? —Like him. You can always tell the Christians because their backyards are full of dirt that's just spaded—so much they have to bury back there." What she said wasn't aimed at me. The anger spilled from something tipped full inside her. For a moment she seemed to have forgotten I was in the room, and then she looked up at me once again, and something softened. "And he is alive today yet—your father?"

"He's dying of cancer, " I told her.

"That's nothing of my doing," she said.

"I didn't blame you," I told her. "I didn't come here to blame you for anything—"

"How many others like you—brothers and sisters?"

"Three—I'm the oldest."

"America?" she asked.

"He left Canada—he had relatives in the States, in South Dakota." I didn't know the story exactly, but I played what I knew against her. "Probably soon after you left him," I said. Something of the defiance had drained from her face. "And you're back here in Holland?" I asked.

She circled the empty chair and then held both points of the back. "I got what I deserved," she said. "I got what I had coming. I don't think God is who the Christians think he is, but there is a God in heaven." She smiled. "I left your father," she raised her hands, rubbed a palm, "and my war lover left me—not even two years. Never married either. Not that I cared." Then she looked at me. "There's a God, I suppose—I just don't like him."

"Maybe it's a woman," I said.

"He's not a woman," she said. "God has a man's heart, as I do."

"Why do you say that?"

"We could never get along—too much alike, me and *God.*" Deliberately she rolled the *g* in the Dutch way. "Women who believe in him *love* God," she told me. "Men who believe respect him. I never loved Him."

"Not even then?" I asked.

"Before the war maybe," she said, reaching for her cup. "Then I was a girl." She pulled it up into both hands but remained standing. "When I was a child, I thought as a child—you know what I mean?"

"And when you knew my father?" I asked.

"I was no child. After the war, there were no children left." She stopped quickly. "Well, maybe your father—I don't know. But none of the rest were children—"

"Nonsense," I said. I wanted to grab her—I really did. "You went winging off to Canada after some war hero? You lied with your body to my father for some pipe dream—to chase some guy in a uniform—and you say you weren't a child?"

She stood straight and tall behind that chair, the cup in both hands, and smiled, then laughed. "You're not like him," she said. "You're not like him at all, are you?"

"How do you know?" I said. "How long were you married? —A week?"

At that moment it hit her for the first time that I hadn't been lying to her, that the man she'd once married under pretext, the man she'd hauled on to some straw mattress somewhere in order to cover her sin, the man she had slept with, only to reach her baby's father in Canada—at that moment she understood that this man she didn't know at all had never even suggested her existence to me. She looked at me and said, "You don't know, do you?"

"I honestly don't know," I told her. "I don't know a word of the story. You're a revelation. Before yesterday, I had absolutely no idea there ever was a Berendina Janssens-Versteeg —no idea."

In little more than ten minutes, I'd seen iron resolve, an arrogance that angered me, and now something close to defeat—all of it so clearly written on her face that she never had to speak at all. I've seen that before in Dutch people—eyes that mirror every splintered emotion from the soul—concrete conviction to abject helplessness. What's going on inside appears so openly on their faces that I wonder what immigrant experience altered that characteristic in so many of the Dutch who left this country, my father included. Dena Janssens never ever would have buried the secret my father did. Why?

And then, just as quickly, those eyes softened once more. She pressed her lips together, then smiled, softly. "You could have been my son," she said. Gentle smile—even adoring. "Maybe I would have liked your mother."

"No," I said. "Not really."

"Why so?"

"The older I've become," I told her, "the more I believe his marriage was not what he wanted us to believe it was. He is a good, good man, but he is capable of falsehood, for righteousness' sake."

"I believe that," she said.

"He was happy in the barn—a different man in the house," I told her.

"What is she like?"

"She's gone. She died five years ago. He's alone." I pushed back the chair from the table, and just for a moment as I looked down at that hiding place beneath me. "My mother," I said, "is as difficult to describe, as she was hard to love." I wasn't tailoring my words. "No one would deny that. But he never complained—I never heard about you, nor about her—never."

Determined smile, sympathetic, even stoic. "It is an act of faith," she said, "to withstand pain—and acts of faith count with the Lord." She bowed her head for a moment, seemed almost sad. "Bloody Christians all swear by election but work their heads off chasing righteousness for a reward they think they're winning all the same."

But she didn't know my father. He is not arrogant, not boastful; he is not puffed up. He may have faults, but he has never chased righteousness for any reason other than personal happiness and service to God—what he would call, simply, "thanks."

"So, you—" she said, and sat down once again beside me, "where do you fit in all of this?" She pulled the chair up close, leaned both her arms over the table towards me. "If you're not your mother's child and you're not your father's boy, then where did you come from—you historian? —"

Every word was measured and cut sharply to fit a path. I will admit it now. In a way, in those few moments in that old house, I loved her for her deliberateness, the way she cut to the quick, so much unlike my father, who seemed to me then to be living—and dying—in a completely different world. She had told me that she was too much like God to love him, and in a way I believed her. Not for a moment did she fritter away the words she could have chosen. I watched her moods shift like wind in the moods in her eyes. Everything was at the surface—nothing hidden away like my father.

"Where did you come from?" she'd asked me.

And I answered her in her own way—unflinching, direct.

"Where did you?" I said. "Where do any of us come from?"

"From the air we breathe," she said. "All this genetics is just so much wasted science," she said. "I am a child of the war, the third child, second daughter, of Hendrick and Berendina Janssens. I was raised in their home—this one. But the war made me what I am." She sat back once again. "You would not believe what this place was like back then." Her arms spread instinctively. "It was a railroad station in here–people coming and going. Resistance people. Three Jews in the barn," she pointed to the back, "three pilots in the *mooie* room." Behind me, a closed door. *Onderduikers* in and out and in and out." Her hands twisted and whirled and jigged. "And my parents–they were like your father, so naive. I sometimes think my father heartily believed that some great dome of grace protected this house." She looked at me directly, silent. "I hated him for that, really–for his innocence. It is a curse to be born of innocent, Christian parents–a curse. And all that time, me and my Canadian were making love–"

"Where?" I said. "With everybody in this house, where did you find a place?"

She laughed. "The great tragedy," she said, "is that we die–and before that grow old." She was back in this house, fifty years before. "For everything that happened–for what I did to your father and what that big-time hero did to me, for all of my parents' innocence, and the craziness," she laughed to herself, "–and the craziness of all of those people and outside the Nazis capable of killing us all." She shook her head. "With everything that happened to me since–my children, who knows where, and your father, and being forced to come back here to Holland–for those months at the end of the war and that man, that Canadian, I'd probably do it all again." She raised a hand toward me. "You'll never understand that, but you asked, 'Where did we make love'? And my answer, Professor Versteeg, is where didn't we?"

"It was war—people were killed, millions," I said.

"And you," she said. "Did you ever know love? —You and your wife?"

"I'm divorced," I told her.

"I don't care," she said. "What I asked you was did you ever know love?"

"As a child?"

"Have you ever known love?" she said, slowly, as if pronouncing the words to an idiot.

"I don't know," I said.

"Then you haven't." Her fingers peaked as she held her hands up in front of her face. "For six months of my life, I had all I could do to breathe it in—in the middle of all of that bombing and Nazis all over, I was in love."

"Seventy-some years," I said. "And that's all the longer it was—six months?"

She raised her finger, pointed. "I was born in 1929, more than a decade before Hitler came to the Netherlands, but I am a child of the war."

"My father?" I said.

"You know him."

"Not like you did."

She nodded at me as if to say I deserved what she was about to say. "A good man. Not handsome. A Christian—but not a damned hypocrite—never a hypocrite." She touched her finger to her lips, sat there for a moment, thinking. "Of course, I used him, and I remember those nights, too. But I had to—my body told me I had to, and my soul said it too. I remember feeling his body on mine, in mine—and all that time I kept telling myself that when we got to Canada, the moment we get to Canada—." She made a bundle in her hands. "I can't say that what I did haunts me, because it's all now so far behind, but I remember him loving me—yes, here on this farm. I lied myself before. I had to make him think the child already there was his. And I remember wanting to cry, not for him, but for my burden of having to deceive a good man, a man I didn't love." She looked at me, shook her head. "I don't expect your sympathy."

"You *never* loved him?"

"I couldn't let myself love him, even if I wanted to. Heaven was in Ontario, Canada. All I wanted was heaven."

"What did he say when you left him?"

"I never told him."

"You mean you simply walked away?"

"In a letter," she said. "I left him a note three days after I left that horrible farm. Three days. I told him the whole story and that he shouldn't come after me because I'd known what I wanted from the day he'd come here to this back door. I'd known exactly what I wanted." She looked at her open hand, as if there were some scar there, something telling; then she raised it to her face, wiped at the corners of her eyes. "In Canada, I simply disappeared—as if it were still the war. I left him, two weeks after we first put down our feet in over there, and I went to find my lover and hero."

She looked up at me, her eyebrows raised, not so much a smile on her face, but something endearing pulled from a corner of her heart she'd not opened before. "You should not have come," she said. "Maybe even your father would say it—we can get by in this world from day-to-day if we don't have to remember some things."

"My father would say there's forgiveness," I told her.

"Yes, he would," she said.

She sat there at her table, alone in a house with more history than a place should have, and for the first time something unburdened within her threatened the strength of what had kept her energized, alive. Maybe they were not so much different, I thought—my father and this first bride.

"I hadn't even thought about that time," she told me. "I hadn't even thought of your father for years—and years. He was gone."

"I'm sorry," I said.

"And so am I," she said, nodding. "And so am I."

Something broke, something stiff and unyielding and very, very beautiful. For the first time, grief came over her eyes like a shadow. "You tell him that, Professor Versteeg," she said. "You tell your father that before he dies—you tell him Dena Janssens is sorry for what she gave him—that pain."

I hadn't gone to that house like the prophet Nathan, to exact some penitence. When I'd come up the lane, I didn't know even the barest outline of the story. But when I left, I'd come to learn more than I'd ever guessed I would. I understood that what she'd told me she wanted my father to know was not only something painfully torn from her own stubborn and courageous heart, but also something my father would want very much to hear—not for himself, not simply to staunch a festering wound of unrequited love. Both of them were beyond that. But my father the Christian would want to know what she'd told me because it would enable him to leave this earth with hope for his first bride, accounts settled. He would want to know that she'd said what she said, not for his sake, but for hers, this woman he probably loved so much he couldn't speak of the pain she'd given him for the rest of his life, pain he'd likely tried hard to cover with love.

What I've come to believe, now, as I drive back to my father's South Dakota farm, is that this burden of history I've unearthed, this story will be a gift I can bring to his last days on earth. It will not be unsettling, a nightmare arising from ashes long grown cold and blown away in the countless seasons of prairie winds he's endured on land many would question was meant for anything other than buffalo. The story of Berendina Janssens will give him peace.

I know exactly how he will take the news because I know that what he sees before him now is an honored appointment with the King of Kings. His final journey began two years ago with the discovery of his cancer. Death has been made flesh in his ravaged body, and while he always knew he was going to die, since he's discovered how, his stoic sense of *when* has only deepened his assurance.

And if I can't give to him what he really wants—something of his son's clean and clear commitment to the Lord he himself has served through so much of a loveless life—I can at least bring him this last gift, the broken heart of a woman who once broke his, but more than that, the penitence of another sinner, one he knew intimately and yet not, a woman he slept with and thought he knew, just as fully as he is known. This historian who happens to be his son is very grateful that he can make this one last road straight for the coming of his Lord.

Today I will see my father. We will sit on the deck of the house where I grew up, a place my mother left five years ago. We'll look out on the empty barn he ritually visits three times a day to feed a multitude of cats, the only animals left. We'll sit on chairs beside the geraniums he keeps up on the railings, the sweet smell of life redolent in the air all around us, just as it was on that small farm just outside the Veluwe.

I'm on my way to tell him something he will savor. When I went to the Netherlands, I wondered whether I should even leave the continent with my father in the condition he was. I went with no motive other than something professional and academic. But I have become, by grace alone, a prophet of joy, and for that I thank my father's God, for he has entrusted the great blessing of healing to me, someone who has doubted His goodness and mercy for many years.

My father has been ready to die for a long, long time. But today, maybe for the first time, his son, who has given him great pain in many years of questioning and doubt, is finally ready for him to leave.

Vital Signs

I know my father didn't worry about the kid. Neither did I. He used to say, "Show me a kid who doesn't take a hit somewhere through life, and I'll show you the exception to the rule."

Almost thirty years ago he put a scar like a zipper on his right leg, ankle to the knee. He ran up the grain elevator to check the bin without turning the thing off–that's what he told me, and then he'd say, "That's how you learn, Carl–you get scars." That elevator chain chewed up his pants leg and started on his thigh. My brother Mike shut it down or today my dad would be a cripple.

"You learn things," he'd always say. "That's how life works. You take your licks. You get scars." That's what he'd tell me. I know he didn't worry about the girl.

There was this accident right out in front of his place last night. He lives in town now, moved off the farm already five years ago, maybe more. Time flies. He never heard the sound of a kid getting hit by a car before, but he says he knew it the moment it happened: brakes squeal, shrieking metal, and then this thump that can only be something soft as a body—it all adds up to something you know by instinct. Right in front of his place.

So right away when he heard it, he went outside and the girl is out cold on the pavement, and her bike's got a front wheel that's warped bad. When the kids aren't yours, he says, your thinking is a whole lot clearer since you spend less time wishing you were in their skin—that's what he told me. So right away he determined not to move that child, because my brother Johnny fell through the hay chute once, head first, when he was twelve, and for a long time I know my folks were sure he was going to be a step and a half behind. But he's okay today. Accountant, of all things—numbers. Had more sense than the rest of us and left the farm.

But my father never forgot that day in the barn. "You shouldn't' a moved that boy, Clarence," Doc said to him the day Johnny fell. "You should have left him there just where he was." A dozen times I heard that story. So he didn't move this little girl, just sat beside her and took her head in his hands to keep it off the cold pavement. That's when I showed up.

She was maybe Sandy's age, our youngest—long skinny legs—and she's got a gash on her calf, a healthy one that I figured was going to take a needle and thread. I just happened to be stopping over there about then, and I see all the commotion on the corner. There he was, my father, talking to this little girl, who's woozy.

"You be still now," he said, as if she was hearing him.
Then he cocks his head as if to tell me that she'd taken a good one on the noggin.

Not until then did I see who it was that hit the kid. It was Lenore–that's right, Lenore Sieperda, the very woman my father's been seeing. Her face is all in a blight because of all the fear and hurt she's got in her, what with that little girl lying there, my father's hands around her head. Right away I figured Lenore was coming to his place when it happened, and that it couldn't be all that bad because Lenore's never driven that car more than thirty.

"I never really saw them," Lenore says to me, all frantic with her hands.

"That's sometimes the way it goes," I told her. I looked down at the little girl and her eyes are shut tight and her face is drawn and quartered as if she's watching newsreels of everything that just happened, what she probably never saw in the first place. It's scary, is what I'm saying–any time you take a hit to the head, it's scary.

"Is she going to be all right?" Lenore said.

There sat my father with this little girl and an old woman who found a place in his heart asks him a question like that. You grow up on a farm place like I did and somebody's always hurt, you know? You just can't take it too seriously–maybe that's why I lied, because the fact is, I thought right away that this little girl got stung bad. But I didn't say it–maybe I should have. "Sure," I says, "she's going to be just fine, Mrs. Sieperda."

And then my father says, "Listen, Lenore—you just go over to that chair in my front yard and sit." He said it nicely.

The cop comes. I don't know the guy right off. From where I'm squatting on the pavement beside the little girl, he's big and he's too young, but I think that a lot. He's got high cheeks like a Faber, like an Eskimo.

"Where's the ambulance anyway?" I ask him.

"Does anybody know the girl's name?" he says, and just then I hear the siren.

Then everything happens in a rush. Rog Feddars pulls up in his pick-up, jumps out, and leans over beside the kid saying "straight down from the Hy-Vee" to whoever is listening on the other end of the phone he's got in his hand. And, "Let me have the girl, Clarence," he says to my father.

Rog Feddars pulled off a car door with his bare hands ten minutes before they could get the Jaws of Life out to that big accident west of town a couple, three months ago. But here's what happened: my father started to let go of the girl and then he looked down at his hand and he saw what I did–blood.

"She got a laceration back there?" Rog says.

My dad went feeling around for something open. "I don't feel a thing," he told Rog. "Where's it coming from?"

Rog takes that girl's chin in his hand, turns her face slow, and then he points. The blood's coming from her ear. That scared me, but still the little girl's crying and she seems okay. He took the girl from my dad, and the ambulance guys wrapped up her head in gauze and snapped a plastic brace under her chin and around her neck.

Now it turns out the little girl's just moved to town with her family, and nobody recognized her except for the fact that there was two of them, the girl who Lenore hit and her little sister, who's pint-sized and everybody forgot about in all the action. Finally, that little one steps up out of nowhere and says her name and somebody calls her folks' place from a cell phone.

And that's the story, beginning to end–ten minutes maybe, at most, and just like that she is carted off and all the rest of us stand there on the corner in front of my father's house to tell each other the story time and time again, as if maybe it'll make sense if we go through it often enough. The whole event has my father robbed of words, and that's not something that happens often. But then, Lenore is in on the whole deal in a very scary way.

What I'm saying is, that when those EMTs left, I wasn't worried about the little girl–Lenore's driving, the fact that the kid was seeing us and everything, then what's a little blood? From the ear, sure–that scared me. But it just didn't look all that bad.

My father wasn't saying a thing. He's my dad and I love him, and neither me or Emily was all that keen on his courting again at his age—I don't know why. But I didn't get in his way either—none of us kids did, even if we were sure he was more being courted than courting himself, if you understand what I'm saying. And here she is—Lenore is sitting there on my father's yard, and she still doesn't have her feet on the ground.

"You see it happen?" the tall cop says to me.

"Maybe my father did," I said.

"I heard it," my father told him, "but I never saw it."

"Did anybody?" he says, flipping open his clipboard.

Nobody said a thing. There was a crowd.

"Who was driving the car?" he says.

My father didn't tell him right away. He stalled, is what I'm saying. He wanted to lie—that's why he waited. But he had no choice finally, so he pointed up the sidewalk to where Lenore was standing with her friend Ann's arm wrapped around her shoulders.

We're talking here about two people who are down about all of this, not to mention the child with blood coming from her ear. The kid is on her way to getting taken care of, I'm thinking, but my dad and Lenore Sieperda are bleeding in their own way, and I am too, for everybody.

The thing is, Lenore is worried sick about the girl. Now my dad really likes that woman, which is hard to understand because I guess I'd think that all there is of love would be packed up and put away once you're pointing towards 90. I'm not sure what love is, but I'm very sure whatever it is my father feels for

Lenore isn't exactly what he felt for my mother when both of them were seventeen and altogether too young to get married. It's about companionship, I suppose, which is maybe what it ought to be from the very beginning. Figure love out and you won't work for the rest of your life.

But he knows too well what kind of driver Lenore is. One Sunday afternoon she wiped out half my father's irises when she missed the driveway. He's still got long stripes of crabgrass in his lawn where she rode up the curb. I told Emily that if they get married, my father would have to build a two-car garage just to keep one side standing. She drives like a troubled kid is what I'm saying, and maybe she shouldn't be behind the wheel at all. He knows that.

My guess is that he knew the little girl was hurt—he had her blood on his hands. But he never stopped doing anything for a little blood, not once that I remember. And I know this, too—he knew Lenore was standing over there dying inside. And he didn't like that, no matter what he says. Whenever we talk about the two of them, he says they're just a couple of cutters-and-canners trying to hold on to each other on the kill floor. But Lenore knew what she'd done. She knew it very well. That little girl's blood was on her hands, too. My father had too many things to worry about for someone his age, and I knew it.

I forgot the part about the father. He flies up in a van just as they put his daughter on the gurney and wheel her into the ambulance. He's big as a linebacker, but he doesn't say a word.

So I said to him, "Is there something I can do?"

He slings me the keys to that van and asks if I can pick up the girl's mom. They live over on Park, he says, and I know where it is because I knew Brocks moved out and the place was up for sale for nearly a year because real estate is not moving and hasn't been for a while.

"You just go with," I told him, pointing at the EMT's, "and let me pick her up."

"So he and the little sister get in the ambulance with Rog Feddars and there I stand with his keys—shaking, I don't mind saying. But before I go get that little girl's mom, I got to talk to Lenore because it's clear to me that my dad's not saying much at all."

"You talk to the policeman," I told her. "You tell him what happened—you tell him the truth."

So while they're talking, I drive that van over to the little girls' house, where the garage is full of moving boxes and the girl's mother is standing out front, fretting to beat the band since she hasn't heard a word since her husband left in a storm a minute ago.

"What can you tell me about my daughter?" she asks me, half crying.

She gets the neighbor lady to come over and watch the kids, and I pack her in the van and try to tell her that my own brother once hit his head so bad on our barn floor that my folks wondered if everything would be okay, and he still came out of it well enough to own his own business in Omaha. I don't know what she heard. Most of the time she had to work to hold herself steady.

I drove her over to the hospital in that van, and all the time I was telling her that I was sure her little girl was going to be okay. "She might look a little worse than she is," I told her. "Usually there's blood," I said, "but they come out of it okay." You got to put on the best in times like that because what's in her head is the sheer darkness on the other side of hope. Sometimes even a Christian just has to lie, is what I'm saying.

So there I am at the hospital with somebody else's van and no way to get home, when my dad's fishing buddy Fred appears out of nowhere. He's getting his feet checked by some traveling specialist. He can bring me back, I figure, but I'll be darned if he doesn't know one thing about the accident because it's taken so long for the x-rays of his joints to get done and the specialist is up to his ears in bad feet.

So I told him everything I knew. "She wasn't going fast," I said. "She never goes fast."

"Lenore, huh?" Fred said. I knew he was thinking she and that Taurus of hers should have been parked long ago. Everybody knows that.

"She's not in good shape herself," I told him. "All messed up about it."

"Sure," he says, "I bet." But I know what he was thinking.

Now Fred's not quick on his feet, see. I don't know what it is he's got wrong, but it seems that when you get his age—and my old man's—there's always something. We're walking out to his car when I spot the helicopter coming to take somebody to St. Luke's, and the liar in me says how strange it must have been that our little hospital has two emergencies going on at one time. Then I see the cop and stick two and two together.

"That helicopter's not for the little girl, is it?" I said.

He nods. "I think it'll be all right," he says, and then he asks me again. "You didn't see it happen?"

It's time for more bad news, I thought. "It's the old woman's fault, I guess," I said.

He shrugs his shoulders like a man who doesn't want to stake his ground. "The little girl ran right into the Taurus—you see the dent on the fender? She wasn't watching at all. The little one says they never stopped. It looks like it might have been the kid's own fault."

So I'm thinking it's a miracle, but I'm telling myself there's no reason to feel good about anything with that little girl—who's not much more than a year or two younger than my own little Sarah—and now she's going to be on her way to Sioux City for something bigger than they could handle right here in town.

The cop's eyes look like he's already spent too much time worrying. "They must have come off the sidewalk by your dad's place there and never looked at all," he says. "You know how kids are." He's got the pencil in his hand. "The little one says they never looked."

That's exactly what he said. What I'm saying is, I didn't know how to feel. Lenore—she had to feel better, I'm sure. And my father—I don't know what he might have been thinking. But still there was that little girl.

I told Fred what happened when he was driving me home from the hospital. "Lenore didn't get a ticket," I said.

"Wasn't her fault?" he said.

"Seems not," I told him.

He pursed his lips like a man who's got too much sour apple.

He let me off in the front of my dad's house, where the Taurus had been parked. I'd pulled up along the lindens on the north side. And that's when I saw it. That cop said those two little girls were coming off the sidewalk on the north side. He said they didn't look and ran right into the Taurus. He said, "You know how kids are."

What he never noticed is that my father has no full sidewalk on the north side of the house. He's got a 15-foot spur where somebody put in sidewalk years ago, the chunk that would have eventually fit between the east side sidewalk and the rest, but the rest never got laid. What I'm saying is the little girls weren't on the sidewalk at all. The little girls were on the street, not the sidewalk, because there isn't a full sidewalk there. That young cop must have never really seen that at all, never looked that closely. He was thinking they came off a sidewalk that was only a spur. Good night, I'm saying to myself. Your young men shall see visions and dream dreams.

I went in the house. Lenore had gone home, and my father was there alone, sitting down at the kitchen table, nothing in front of him, just sitting there. That's all right too, I thought, because right then I wasn't anxious to talk about things I thought I knew better than he did.

Rog Feddars called and I picked up the phone, because my father sat there stone-faced. I'm not even sure whose pain he's feeling between his ribs. Rev. Jacobs, Rog says, took the Mom and Dad to Sioux City in their own van. Rog says they're all down there and it doesn't look as if the little girl's out of the woods yet, but all he knows is her vital signs were strong enough for her to fly in that helicopter, and that's good, he says. That was the first decent news since I heard the chopper. What I'm saying is, I didn't know who to feel more awful for.

"Dad," I said, "I think she's going to be all right."

Like I said, it's not like my father to be without words. But he sat there speechless at the kitchen table with a pile of junk mail a foot thick in front of him because he says he likes it–gives him something to read. He must have just picked it out of the mailbox.

"Who?" he says.

"The little girl," I said. He didn't even know about the airvac. I hadn't told him. "They took her to St. Luke with the helicopter," I said.

Then he looked up.

"But she's going to be all right."

"More'n a little bump?" he said.

"More'n a little bump, I guess, but she's going to live," I told him.

"Going to live?" he said, as if it weren't something he'd even considered. "She's going to live, you say?–She going to be a little off or what?" he asked me.

"Nobody knows," I said.

My father looks peculiar when he thinks. Everything goes into a stall, slow motion or something, and he does these lip things, almost calisthenics, moves his lips around his mouth as if he has no teeth, which he does. "There's always Johnny, you know–your brother," he said.

"I know. I know," I told him. "He came out of it fine as anything."

"You're not lying?" he said.

"She's already there, probably," I told him, looking up at the clock above the sink.

"Lenore was coming here, you know?" he said. "She was coming here to see me."

"I figured as much."

"That makes me responsible too, I guess, don't it?" He brought up his left hand and smoothed back his mustache, as if his twitching lips had to be held down.

Sometimes I look at my father and I can't help but think how much different we are, the two of us, even though people say I'm his spittin' image. What do I know about horses, for example? What do I know about all those changes he's seen in his life? This world is not his own anymore, powerful a man as he was. And always a talker.

Once we were out in South Dakota, at the Hills, where all those buffaloes roam, and there we were, Emily and me and the kids, right in the car, right in the middle of the herd. And an old one, an old gray-furred one walked up on to one of those faraway hills, just walked off from the herd, and I told myself he was going to die. He was just walking away so as not to make himself a burden. That old one, his life was over. It was time for him to leave.

Some part of me doesn't like the idea of Lenore hanging around my dad, but another part says maybe it'll keep him from leaving the herd himself and moving up like an old bull over the hills west of town, walking out there alone until he gets to the river.

"You know she didn't get a ticket?" he said.

"I heard," I told him.

And then he looked at me in a way I don't remember him ever looking at me before, begging. I know what he wanted me to say, but I wasn't going to give it to him because I'm not comfortable telling my father how to take care of his problems.

"Those girls must have just run right out in front of the car," he said.

I thought for a minute what I could say right then. I thought about it because I didn't want to shrink either. "Maybe so," I said. "Could well be," I told him. "I wasn't there."

"That's what the law said," my father told me, pointing out front as if the cop were still investigating, which he should have been. He shrugged his shoulders.

"If that's what the law says," I told him, "then that's what must have happened, I guess."

"I guess," he said.

And then all around was the kind of silence that's in that house all too often now that he's alone, the kind of silence my father lives with, big talker like he always was.

"You don't need me, right?" I said.

"What would I need you for anyway?" he said. "I'm old enough to vote."

"Sure you are," I said.

He pulled his glasses away from his face and rubbed at the sore spots on his nose. "I ought to get a new pair, but I figured these would last me," he said.

"What's a pair of glasses cost?" I said. "You go get them, you hear?"

"Seems a waste," he said.

"You're no waste, Dad," I said.

"Like throwing money out the window," he told me.

"Emily and I don't need money," I told him. "You know that."

Then he put them back on. "Just rub every once in awhile and it goes away, like everything else," he said. "Who knows how much, too–$125 or more for a new pair."

"Big deal," I told him.

And then he said it. "Wasn't her fault," he told me.

"Lenore?"

"No, that little girl," he said. "Wasn't her fault at all."

He didn't need me to tell him as much.

We don't say much for a while. He's all in a stew, and I'm thinking I didn't have to say anything that was already ringing up in his mind. We sat there for a time, and it was right about then she showed up, Lenore did. She rang the bell at the front door. Now we were way in the back of the house, and I didn't know who it was, but I walked along with my father toward the front door when

I saw her standing there, and I told him–before he even opened the door–I told him that I didn't have to be there and I was going home, and he said–without even looking at me, as if he didn't want her to know that I'm there–he said, "You're not leaving. I need you here." That's what he said. "Just get out in the kitchen somewhere," he said, "because this ain't going to be easy."

He wanted me to hide, so I did. I went out through the kitchen, stayed out of sight, and became a witness to everything that happened between those two. I went to the family room, which is an odd way of saying it because my dad has no family there with him anymore. But for a minute I stepped back there because I knew he wanted me in the house but out of the way.

My mother's picture is out there on a rack of books and magazines, most of them hers since my father never read much at all in his life until now. My mother died on the farm. For years she wanted him to get off and get a place in town, and finally she just died while he was in the barn. He came walking in from chores and found her in the sewing room. He knew she was gone the minute he saw her, he said. The ambulance came out and they tried, but all for naught.

That was the only time in my life I saw my father cry–and that was when he told me he was leaving the farm. "Farming don't owe me a cent anymore," he said, "and all it was me being scared of leaving that place–that's what kept me out there anyway in the last couple of years, when me and your mother should have already been in town. Frieda would have loved that." Then he turned away because he didn't want me to see the tears. "Truth is," he said, "I just as well as killed the woman I loved by not listening to her. I was lying to myself and staying out there only because I was flat scared to change, old and scared. I thought I wouldn't know what to do with myself if I wasn't walking out to the barn three times a day." That's what he told me, out in the shed, when he told me two months after she'd died that he was moving to town alone. For her, I thought, even though she never had the joy.

I don't know what he and Lenore talked about for a while because I was out of ear range, and I liked it that way. I didn't hear anything that I shouldn't have or that I should have either, for maybe ten minutes, and it was just getting to me then that I didn't care for this kid's game, sitting back there as if I were a secret, when the phone rang. I picked it up myself, but before I did I yelled to tell him I would–and to make Mrs. Sieperda know that I was, in fact, in the house. "I got it," I said, way too loud. Lenore doesn't hear well either.

It was the pastor's wife. She said everything was going to be fine. "Angela" that little girl's name was Angela–I could have figured as much–she's got a fracture, the preacher's wife says, and it's not so good, but they've got her in stable condition. That's the gist. "She's going to be okay," she said. "You can tell your father so." There was that at least. That one was over. The kid was going to be okay.

So I had to tell both of them, but maybe Lenore more than my father because she had to be worried sick, even more than my dad. So I walked into the front room and there the two of them were sitting, on the couch, almost snuggling–two old cutters and canners, like he says. Their eyes were still red, both of them, even though Lenore's are in tougher shape than his.

"Everything's going to be fine," I told them. "I got a call from the pastor's wife, and she says the girl's going to stay on there at St. Luke's–"

"They took her to Sioux City?" Lenore says.

I looked at my father, who stuck out his chin like a martyr.

"Pretty much standard procedure with a bump on the head," I told her. That was a lie too.

"Oh, my God," she says and down goes her face. "I wish I'd have known. I been praying hard, and I didn't even know," she said. "I couldn't even drive home. Ann Wanders was with me. She was shaking too. She drove me back. I haven't thought about a thing except–"

"Well," I said, trying to make it all okay, "it's one of those things that happens."

"But she's okay?" she says, and once again I told them what the preacher's wife had told me.

Both of them breathed in deep. I figured maybe we were out of this.

"You know," Lenore said, "they never stopped for me at all—I was going to turn down your street there, and they were on the sidewalk and never stopped—they never even slowed down."

The cop convinced her, too. Lenore never looked down at the sidewalk either. She got hit herself, just out of nowhere. She'd never seen the kids coming, but they weren't on any sidewalk. They were on the street and the whole accident was her fault. She should have seen them. It was that simple. And my father knew. And then I wondered, really, whether love really mattered when it came to truth, or whether truth mattered much when it came to love.

"If I could have done something," she said, "but they never even saw me—the cop said as much."

"They came off the sidewalk, did they?" my father said.

He knew. He knew.

"They came right off that sidewalk and never even looked."

And then he looked at me.

"They never waited a second," Lenore says, a hanky crumpled up in her fist. "The policeman said it himself."

"Did you see them coming?" I said.

"I think we both did," she told me, and she sat back. "I'm just so happy that she's going to be okay. I couldn't have been going fast, Clarence," she said to my father. "You know how I drive."

I said to myself, "Honey, I know how you drive."

"I started to turn toward your place and they never even stopped." She lets out this big breath as if she's been saving it since the accident. "They're new in town, too, I heard. Imagine that. Just in town and then that kind of accident." She twists her head all around as if there was someplace in the room she could put her eyes and forget that girl banging off the side of her Taurus. "I saw her dad there, you know, and now she's at St. Luke's?"

What I'm wondering is what my father's going to say. "You know how kids are," he's likely to say. "Broken leg today, good as new tomorrow. That's how you learn—you get scars." But it s all serious on his face. He draws up his chin as if the starch in the collar of his church shirt is starting to bind, and I don't know what he's going to do.

"I can't tell you what I felt. I'll hear that sound forever," she said. "I'm just sick, Clare—just sick." She pulls her fist up to her face and chews on that wet hanky.

I wonder—I really do—if he's going to let this go.

"They would have taken my license if I'd got a ticket," she said. "I just know that they would have—somebody our age."

Our age, she says.

"I'm just so happy it's not my fault."

I wish she hadn't said that.

"I *need* that car," she said. "I go so slow I never harm anybody." Plain old self-defense, will to live we all got that's sometimes dead wrong, capable of deceit. I know it. I got it too. It's amazing, what we'll excuse if we're the ones to pay the piper.

And all this time Dad's never said a thing. There we sit, the three of us—the woman he loves—if that's what you call it—lying even to herself; and me, my father's son, who knows the unvarnished truth as well as he does. And my dad, trying to find some kind of balance, like we all do.

"They never stopped, Clare—they never even looked, I'm sure," Lenore says.

Just cause you're old doesn't mean people have to lie to cover up. Then you might as well be dead. That's what I'm thinking. Of course, I've never been all that thrilled with the pursuit this woman put on my old man either. Maybe I'm prejudiced. Maybe I can't be trusted either.

"I'd be just sick if it was my fault," she says. "I'm just sick anyway, Clare," she says. "You saw where they hit the car too—on the side."

My father nodded as if he saw her car right there beside the love seat.

"Ann said it too—they never stopped, Clare—they never even looked, I'm sure," Lenore said. Then her eyes go down and she starts to fidget on that chair and I'm just sure she knows, too, else she wouldn't have to say it a thousand times.

The thing is, I saw the blood on my father's hands. I knew what had happened, and I saw that little girl, just a year younger, maybe, than my own. I know what kind of sidewalk we're talking about here.

"It wasn't my fault, Clare," she said again. "They hit *my* car," she said. "You saw it yourself. Even that young policeman said it wasn't my fault," she says to me, "and it wasn't."

Then he looks up at me, looks me straight in the eye like he's done a thousand times, only this time he's asking, not telling.

I shrugged my shoulders.

And that's when he let the horse out of the barn. "I think maybe, Lenore, you ought to reconsider here," he said, "because it was too your fault." Hushed–he spoke in a hushed tone, but the words went out there like bats that somehow sneak indoors.

She right away straightened up and gets like we all do–she throws her shoulders back. "What'd you say?" she said.

I've seen him herd hogs and lose his cool so bad he turned half animal himself, but this time he was very careful. "There's got to be a place for the truth, Lenore," he told her. "It *was* your fault, and the both of us know it."

Her face changed to something hard and dark as sin.

"Those kids didn't come off my sidewalk," he told her. "I don't have sidewalk east and west on my yard. There's no sidewalk there for them to ride down."

"But the policeman says–"

"There's only the lindens, Lenore–biggest, most beautiful trees in the whole town. I wouldn't cut 'em down for no sidewalk."

She sat there fretting with her fingers until she knew she had to say something, poor woman. "It wasn't my fault," she said again, her face down and back to weepy. "Don't I have enough to cry about? Why are you saying this?"

"I get no delight out of hurting you, Lenore," he told her. "But I don't know myself that you should be driving anymore."

What I saw on her face was despair. The sad part was, that woman probably needed my father more right then than anytime. She needed him to take her in his arms.

"You think you're higher than the law," she said. "That's what you think all right. The police themselves told me it wasn't my fault. How do you think you know better?" And then she lets out a spiel I don't have to repeat here because not everything people say when they're angry comes out of the better end.

My father took it all, everything she threw at him. I think he figured it was no use to spill more blood here.

So she leaves. Not in a huff. People her age can't move in a huff. It takes awhile, but neither of them say a word, and I didn't either.

My father looked more tired, more hurt, than I've seen him since that day in the shed when he told me he was leaving the farm.

"You call me, Lenore," he told her at the door. "Soon enough you're going to cool off and you'll get some sense back.

When you do, you call me, hear?" That's what my father said as he stood there holding the door open.

Lenore never looked back.

"I'll be here," he told her as she was ambling down the walk. "You listen—I'll be here."

My father could have gone to that cop and showed him there is no sidewalk, but it seemed to me that his way of doing this wasn't going to leave the kind of scar the whole public business would have, a trial and her name in the paper and what not else. And even if it does leave something ugly on that woman, this way at least it'll be on her in a place nobody but the two of us will ever see. That's what he's thinking, I'm sure.

But I've never seen my father so quiet. He walks right past me as if I'm not even there.

"You did the right thing," I told him, but he went into the kitchen to fetch coffee, plugs in the pot, and then looks up at me. "I got cleaning up to do outside," he said.

I was thinking I ought to stay for at least awhile. Emily was going to wonder where I was, but I figure he's my dad.

There are kids out front. He must have seen them from the door. They're sitting in a circle on their infernal mopeds with their lights down on the pavement to see where that little girl's blood lies stark naked in two pools. My father stepped out there on the porch and yelled so loud that someplace the next day I'm sure those boys went out of their way to talk about the old geezer who threw a fit when they weren't doing nothing but staring down at blood and cold pavement.

I went along with him to the street. He hauled out the hose because he thought that what that little girl left on the pavement had likely been stared at long enough in one night. I helped him unroll the garden hose all the way from the spigot on the south side, and then he let that pavement have it, I'll tell you. He stood there for five minutes washing away blood till nothing but two light shadows still lay there between tar stripes, two shadows that weren't going to go away all that easy, blood being what it is, so much of us in it.

I don't watch much television. I'm sitting there in my dad's family room ten minutes later, and the wall clock's making all the noise either of us need to hear. I tried reading a church paper to settle my nerves, but it didn't work, and I'm figuring how much easier it would have been just to let sleeping dogs lie, how dumb it was maybe, how righteous some people might think it was to assume we had to straighten out things ourselves, as if we know the whole truth.

My father's not saying anything. He knows she's awake. He knows Lenore's not sleeping and she's a bundle of nerves somewhere. He knows that woman, and he wishes like heck she'd call, because with the two of us not talking right then, I get a sense too of just how quiet it can be in that house, and how quiet he knew it was in hers, even though both of them are in the middle of town.

That's what I'm thinking, with the sound of that old clock wearing away on the wall a room away, and that's when I tell him I have to leave, him waiting for a call from a woman who just might not. I told him I had to leave because Emily would be worrying by this time since I'd told her I was only going to stop over at his place for a couple of minutes.

"I don't need you," he said, like a kid.

That was a lie too.

So I went home and told Emily this whole story, and there the two of us sat in our kitchen nook, shaking our heads and worried sick because it's late as anything, far too late for an old man like him to be up sitting beside the desk, unable to read or watch a minute of television, just sitting there, squirming around on his desk chair, not getting comfortable a bit, sitting there like a teenage kid all alone beside the phone, waiting forever for some wonderful call, some kid just like one of ours.

And us too, waiting for him and for her, the two of us right there beside the phone.

Casa Mia

From the third floor balcony, Reverend Martin Fleet looked down into the very heart of Casa Mia Apartments, where some young thing lay on her stomach at poolside, one foot up behind her waving a dangling sandal. The woman was obviously looking for more than a tan, and she was getting it. His handsome son-in-law, Gabe, stood beside her, chest-deep in the water, scrubbing scum from the tiles at the water line, giving her eyes he never flashed at his own wife.

You could see it all from three floors up. Any Old Testament prophet worth his salt would have called it the hanky panky it was. Even though every last thing on her body could have been stored in a box of Band-Aids, it wasn't her nakedness that drove a stake into the old preacher's heart, it was the music between them, the kind of music he hadn't heard between Gabe and his own daughter for a minute in the two days' he and his wife had been visiting.

Years ago he remembered seeing one of his own deacons chatting on a public telephone in a mall. From the rapture on his face, Martin knew the man was in trouble. That's what he told Sarah, his wife—blessed few married people showed faces full of that much glee, he'd said. Sarah was mad, but he'd been right. If Sarah saw the goings-on at pool; she'd see it here too, he thought, clear as the hand in front of your face. But Sarah was inside with Donna.

For a moment, he thought about hurling down the Budweiser bar lamp he'd picked up from the vacated apartment he'd been cleaning, flinging it like Moses from the mountain. He had to say something. Gabe was his daughter's husband. "Did you wait an hour?" he yelled down, trying to be cute.

Gabe looked up and cupped a hand behind his ear. Then the girl said something, and he leaned back and laughed. "Cara says waiting an hour is an old wives' tale, Pops—besides, I'm not even swimming."

Chest deep in the water and he's not swimming, Martin thought. He who sups with the devil had best use a long spoon. "Well, I'm not going in after you if you cramp up," Martin told him, as he started down the first flight of stairs. "Maybe she will."

Gabe thumbed at her. "She's the lifeguard," he said, and the young woman smiled.

"In that case, maybe I ought to pull a suit on myself," he said. "Got anything else for an old preacher to do? – I got 314 sparkling."

Gabe was in so deep he had to hold to the side of the pool like a barnacle.

"Get us some warmer weather," the girl said, pulling herself up from the chair.

"You tell her I could do miracles?" he said from the first landing. "I'm retired."

Gabe said something quietly to the woman, then shaded his eyes and turned to look back up at him. "I told her you had connections in high places," he said.

Connections was what Gabe wanted, but not in high places. The girl pulled a robe around her and reached down to pick up a book. Dark hair, the figure of some babe on TV. She weighed a ton less than did Donna, who was pregnant again. She dropped her lotion into one of the pockets of the robe, then went over to where Gabe was scrubbing, stuck a toe in the water, and told him a few more goodies.

"She need something fixed I can handle?" Martin yelled.

"Her name's Cara," Gabe told him. He pointed across the court. "Lives in 256–she's from Minnesota, like you."

"That so?" he said. "Whereabouts?"

"Edina," the girl said.

Figures, he thought–little rich girl. She leaned over and told Gabe a couple more things while cupping a handful of water like those iffy Israelite troops Gideon left behind when he went into battle.

"I didn't chase you off, did I?" Martin said.

"I'm a nurse," she told him. "Got to work."

Educated too, he thought, coming slowly down the last flight, one hand on a rail, one on the beer lamp. She ought to know better. But he had a sixth sense about Arizona. He and Sarah had been to Phoenix twice before to visit Gabe and Donna, but already that first time he'd worried about his daughter in a place like this where people walk around half naked so much of the year, especially when what lay behind Donna's last ten years was no a path of righteousness. If Gabe was up to something, it wouldn't be the first time her life would shipwreck–far from it, even though this time the mess wouldn't be at her hands.

When he got down the stairs, Gabe had nearly circled the pool. The man had a body like *David*, Michelangelo's version. Curly head of hair, high cheekbones, blue eyes, sculpted arms and shoulders, not a hint of a paunch–the only flaw on him a long whitish scar that ran around the base of his neck, as if someone, years ago, had tried to lift his head from his chest.

"Got a place for this?" Martin asked, holding up the Budweiser sign.

"Whoa!" Gabe said. "What a prize."

"Whoever lived in 314 didn't think so," he said. "I got a whole laundry bag full of Budweiser junk—sunglasses, hats, decks of cards."

"You know," Gabe said, "you ought to come along with me Sunday. It's about time to empty the closet at the flea market down at the track."

"The track?" Martin said.

"Dog track—down by the river."

Sunday—sure, he thought, *down at the dog track when he ought to be at church*. Martin's own father, the preacher, would not have believed his granddaughter's husband was down at a gambling joint on the Sabbath, selling fancy beer lights and whatever other rubble booty renters left behind. But then, his father wouldn't have believed a lot about this granddaughter—two kids from different fathers, a third on the way, her family in a two-bedroom apartment those kids rarely stepped out of, occupied as they were most of the day by a rack of videos big as a branch library. That his father was dead was a blessing; it would have been difficult for him to forgive the transgressions Donna had already chalked up, more difficult for his father, at least, than the Lord of hosts.

He put the cleaning stuff down beside the party room. "Fancy woman, that," he said, nodding toward the path she'd left on the sidewalk.

"Needs a man, Pops," Gabe told him, "needs one bad." He stopped scrubbing for a minute, brought both hands up on the side of the pool. "Sometimes I think I ought to tend bar. When you do maintenance in a place like this, you hear everybody's blues."

"Like preaching," Martin said, pulling a chair out from under an umbrella. "You hear so many people's problems you forget your own."

"Is that bad or good?" Gabe said.

"That's a kind of lie," he told him. "It's what I told myself for a lot of years." He pointed up the trail of the Minnesota nurse. "Are you one of her options?"

Gabe looked at him in that innocent way Martin never believed was as guileless as it seemed. "Of course not," he said. "I'm a married man."

"If you're fibbing, your nose'll grow."

Gabe looked cross-eyed at the middle of his face, then tweaked his nose. "Nothing there," he said. "Nothing but the truth, so help me God."

"Maybe you're lying to yourself," Martin said.

"Look," Gabe said, "my nose is staying put."

"As long as your heart is," he said.

"The old conscience is clear," Gabe told him.

"Your will can make your conscience sing the song you want it too–"

"I thought your conscience was the voice of God," Gabe said.

"Only when it's up to snuff," Martin told him.

Gabe tossed the plastic brush up on the edge, disappeared for a moment under the water, then put both hands down on the side of the pool and pulled himself up and out. "You ought to write a book, Pops," he said, picking up his towel. "You could get on Oprah. You could make millions."

Pops, he thought–*Pops*. "What I'm saying is, I hope you don't return the look of those cow eyes that Minnesota nurse lays on you," he told Gabe. "Don't break faith with my daughter."

Not for a minute did Gabe stop toweling off. "You think I'm crazy? –She'd kill me." Big happy smile. Then he hung the towel around his waist, tucking in the edges. "I got work to do," he said, and he walked away following those toe prints.

He never knew exactly how to read a man who had really never been to church in his life, a man who pawned beer lamps at a dog track on the Sabbath and could talk so openly yet scare him to the bone.

*

"You're just doing what you always do," Sarah told him when they took a walk down Blaine, past some scraggly citrus trees in the front yards of a row of unkempt houses. Out of earshot of their daughter, he'd told his wife about the Minnesota nurse. "You're doing it again, Mart–," she said, "you're trying to fight your daughter's battles." He had a hold of her hand. "She's not a little girl anymore."

"Right is right," Martin said.

"How do you know?" she said. "Maybe they're just friends."

"That's not what I saw," he told his wife.

"How do you know what you saw is true?"

"I know."

"And that's what I'm supposed to believe? –That you saw your son-in-law talking to some girl in a swimming suit–"

"Hardly a suit–."

"–and you knew right away that they were having an affair?" She jerked her hand out of his and snapped her fingers. "Just like that, you knew?"

"I didn't say it already happened," he said.

"Then stay out of it," she said.

"An ounce of prevention–"

"An ounce of poison. If he tells Donna what you said, we might as well pack up and leave." She stopped where she stood. "She'll have us out of here that fast–you know that, don't you? You remember what she's already said to you in her life. We've been through this before, Mart—just love her, y'hear?"

The whole street was about a decade past redemption, the houses needing paint, the front yards a mess, Whataburger wrappers and soft drink cups all over from the joint down the street. He turned to face her. "I didn't accuse him," he told her.

"How can you say that?" she said. She walked up beside him, took hold of him at both elbows, stared into his face. "Honey, our daughter thinks she's *got* something here—maybe for the first time in her life. She thinks this is something that's going to bring her peace."

"Only one thing's going to bring her any peace—"

"Love," she said. "Don't be judging her again, Mart. What she needs more than anything is just plain love."

"Not truth?" he said.

"But you don't know the truth," she said. "You just *think* you saw something—"

"He told me, Sarah—he told me himself. He's the one who said the woman needed a man."

"And why couldn't you let it go at that?"

Not to say what he did when Gabe told him about that woman's needs would be like denying himself, he thought. "I got to learn to hold my tongue," he said. "Is that it?"

She shook her head sadly. "Can an old dog learn new tricks? Can a leopard change his – "

"You're asking me to deny myself," he said.

"But didn't Christ say the same thing?"

He knew very well what he'd seen and heard, but what he had to do, he thought—what Sarah wanted him to do—was look at a worthless street like this one, full of half-wrecked cars parked on dead front lawns strewn with last year's toast-colored palm fronds, houses with patched roofs and chipped stucco—and *not* try to calculate the elbow-grease it would take to redeem the whole mess. Love, not judgment—that was all. "You're telling me I got to look at things in a whole different way, Sarah," he said.

She bit her lip, then unbuttoned the top button of his shirt. "For our daughter," she said. "What I'm asking is for you bite your tongue for her—and for me?"

Somewhere in Proverbs, he thought—"Reckless words pierce like a sword, but the tongue of the wise brings healing." Maybe she had a point. Of course, Solomon had his problems too—smart man, but no self-control. Should have listened to his own advice.

*

When they got back to Casa Mia, he told Sarah he needed to walk a little more to straighten out the pretzel in his soul. So instead of going inside, he hiked out behind the apartments, past the dumpster at rear door of the electronics store on Thomas Road, then through the bright diagonal lines of the parking lot and right up to five full lanes of insane traffic, where he stood at a spot there really was no place to stand, no sidewalk at all but a parking lot. With all that traffic, a couple thousand people passed him every five minutes, all of them in a hurry, not one of them conscious of his standing there, much less his pain.

He stood there and wondered what kind of life existed here even fifty years ago, Phoenix being so young. He wondered what he would find if he'd simply lift up a layer of city like so much dead skin, roll it back like sod. If he did, he thought, maybe a person could bring something of the desert back here, something of its silence. Right there, across Thomas Road, he'd raze the adult bookstore and put in a garden of organ pipe cactus, tall as monuments, silent as ghosts. He'd take out the strip mall, and put in prickly pear and some elephant ears, a century plant or two in full flower, a couple of little salamanders. Wouldn't it be a finer world? Quieter at least, more silence to hear God whisper in the desert wind.

The cars were a blur. Was a time, years ago when he was a boy, when he knew the features of every last model. Today he couldn't tell a Chevy from a Ford because they all looked alike, especially in Arizona, where most all the cars were white, most of them minivans. And whatever happened to the good old *family* car

He had to stop thinking that way, he told himself, had to stop judging and start loving all this—that's what. He had to start thinking it was God's will that jillions of people migrated to a desert so dry they had to pipe in water just to keep pace. Sarah wanted a place down here herself now that he was retired, a place out of the cold winter, a place somewhere near Donna, her baby, who'd given them, Lord knows, how many headaches already? He had to start believing in progress like every last red-blooded American, had to start thinking that what people needed more of was joy, start singing to the music he'd heard between Gabe and the Minnesota nurse, rather than wishing for a pipe organ rendition of Old Hundredth. He had to glory in love. He was a crotchety old fart. "He who holds his tongue is wise," the Proverbs said after all.

He stood in the middle of the block, cars and trucks and motorcycles rushing by, and remembered the first time they'd come to Arizona to visit–he'd pulled into this very intersection, waiting to make a left on 44th Street, when the light turned red. He assumed he couldn't move, so he didn't–light was red. Any of a dozen Arizona drivers wanted to kill him, the long nose of the Pontiac right in the heart of traffic. Donna said you've got to go on red.

He cut off the corner by walking through the lot of the Mobil station, past drivers pumping their cars full of gas as if the world were made of fossil fuel. *Cut it out*, he told himself. He couldn't think that way anymore, couldn't tell himself there were no sidewalks on Thomas Road because the automobile had crippled people–we don't ride on the trains, they ride on us. Where'd he read that–Thoreau? –And Thoreau wasn't even a Christian. People looked at him strangely. In the city, only bums walked down the street. The homeless.

Maybe that's simply what happens to old people, he thought. They become the homeless because the world is not their home anymore—the next world is. What's left of them gets shoved on reservations like Sun City—give them a golf course to keep 'em out of the way; let 'em talk to each other about bad livers and prostates and swap bad old-people jokes. Dress all their hairless legs in pink shorts so they look like a breed unto themselves.

An air hose on the side of the building hissed like a rattler, a split like a cat's eye right there where the nozzle should have been tight to the hose—a little duct tape will do it, he thought. *Now quit it*, he told himself. Don't think that way, Sarah said. Don't try to fix things always. He had to learn to sit on his tush and play Rummicube. *Love* is the real story of the scriptures, he told himself, but all too often it just wasn't that easy to accomplish in this vale of tears.

If he could walk through the Mobil car wash and clean himself up the way Sarah wanted him, he'd do it in a moment. Walk right through—baptized on 44th and Thomas. Born again. Now he was making fun. Cynicism doesn't become a saint either.

Maybe Sarah's got a point, he said to the Lord, right there at the side of the street. *Maybe it's best to go with the flow.*

Traffic backed up two red lights long, all the way to Blaine. He walked across the parking lot of the 7-11, asking the Lord for patience and love, and that's when he saw Gabe's old truck stuck in a traffic lane; that's when he saw Gabe's sleeveless left arm out of the window, his right arm hung at the wrist over the steering wheel, that sharp white scar inching, snake-like, beneath his left ear; and that's when he spotted the Minnesota nurse just across the seat, her fingers in the curls of Gabe's neck, once again music between them playing louder even than whatever Godless music was blaring inside.

Not more than fifty feet from the place they waited in traffic, he stood and stared because Sarah had said nothing about *not* speaking. He wasn't going to let this pass unnoticed. He stood there and glared, but what was going on in that truck was their whole world and they never gave him a sideways glance. He leered and growled and gnashed his teeth, but all they could see was each other.

He didn't tell Sarah and he didn't tell Donna, and he didn't say a word to his smiley-face son-in-law. A little later, on Donna's request, he opened a meal with prayer, then sat through lunch with his tongue curbed while his own daughter scolded her child unmercifully for leaving her chair for the 123rd time, and never once looked at her husband, nor he at her. Heat between them, he might have taken, but icy cold was far worse. Silent, he worked through the tough crust of a tasteless frozen pizza with a knife and a fork, and acted as attentive as they were to *Wheel of Fortune*,

Sarah's left hand resting menacingly on his thigh. He told himself that he should be happy his kids were learning something, even if it was from a game show. They didn't take a newspaper, left the *Newsweek* he and Sarah had given them for Christmas virtually unopened, and kept six books in the house, four of them Stephen Kings that Gabe claimed ex-renters had left behind and were about to be peddled with the rest of the junk. The other two were romances. At least Donna was reading something, he told himself. Learn to love.

*

That afternoon, his son-in-law put him to work on the barbecues that stood here and there on the grounds. It was a good time to clean them, Gabe said, because in the middle of winter they didn't get much use. They needed cleaning all right, the grates so soiled it was a wonder they hadn't gone up in flame months ago.

Donna came out when he was doing the one behind the party house. She was wearing a halter top that didn't reach over a midriff she would have been better off covered.

His daughter's long string of real-life disasters was legendary, even though he and Sarah had never given up whole. The angel Gabe wasn't the first of her men, after all, and he figured he wouldn't be her last either, now that the Minnesota nurse was making herself available. Donna's late nights had begun already in junior high, drugs following in high school; there'd been one disastrous year in college and then long bouts of joblessness punctuated with on-again, off-again employment at convenience stores, meat-packers, Walmarts, and a string of motels along the Rocky Mountains in Colorado—and he could list only what he and Sarah knew. He'd long ago told himself that what he didn't know about Donna's life wouldn't hurt him.

She came out and wandered around him while he spread foil over the grates of those dirty grills, like Gabe had told him to do. She stalked him, saying nothing, her sandaled feet grating on the lava rock laid in a broad circle around the grill.

Like their two others, Donna was adopted, not quite their own—although he never would have said that around his wife. He'd come to believe years ago that some incendiary devices had been set to flame in her soul by whoever it was that planted her DNA. He and Sarah had had more than their share of trouble with their kids, but then who could blame the children, growing up in a string of parsonages, watched more closely than anybody else's in the small town churches he'd served?

Donna. She was his daughter and he loved her all right, even though there were times when what she'd done to her mother, slaying her with worry, was tantamount to murder.

"Dad," she said, pulling a mop of hair out of her face, "there's something I have to tell you."

He didn't look up. "I don't like the way Gabe told me to do this," he said. "You got a manual? This can't be right."

"What'd he say?"

"He said to put aluminum foil over the grates, shiny side down, and crank up the engine so flames burn the grease." He looked up. "I'm going to blow the place up."

"That's the way he does it–Taylor, get over here," she yelled at her little boy. "Mama didn't say you could go visiting."

Bite your tongue, he told himself. "You and Taylor get back a little," he told his daughter, "or we'll all go to glory together."

"There's something I've been meaning to ask," she said.

She was his beautiful daughter, very dark eyebrows above almost brown eyes and hair that shown an almost violent red. Heavier than she should have been now, but always just a bit too pretty for her own good.

"Taylor!" she yelled, "now you stay around Mom."

"A soft answer turneth away wrath," he said.

"He doesn't hear soft answers," she told him.

"Neither did his mother," he said.

"I'm trying to tell you something, okay? Cut the preaching." She took a fist full of uncombed hair and threw it back over her shoulder.

He dropped the grates, each of them covered in foil, shiny side down, and turned up the gas. "Back off," he said. "The Lord'll take me anyway one of these days, but you got work to do with those little ones." The fire popped inside. "I'm supposed to let it burn for a half hour, full tilt," he said. "Seems like eternity."

"Dad," she said. "I want to know if, some time, I can come home."

He dropped the lid. She knows, he thought. He should have guessed it.

"It's going down the tubes fast—I just know it," she said, looking straight at him. The kid was digging up dirt from the rose bushes, but she let him be. "I mean, between me and Gabe. I don't think it's going to work out."

I don't think it's going to work out—like plans for some family vacation. *It's not a dream—being married*, he wanted to say. *It's work.* "You stay in it," he told her. "You can't run home to Mom again. You got your place."

She never ducked a moment. "All I want to know is that I got someplace to come to—I mean, if it all breaks up. I got to think of the future—with Taylor and Francine—"

Martin pointed at her stomach, "And whatever you got cooking," he said.

Her eyes deepened in a way that had scared him stiff from the time she was a child. "If he goes," she said, speaking of Gabe, "so does this one."

Inside, something nearly snapped, but he bit his tongue. "What's going on?" he said.

"There's somebody else—and it ain't the first time." She turned toward Taylor. "We're going to have to clean those hands," she said. "Go wipe 'em in the pool—you hear me? Go wipe them in the pool."

So much for peeing. "You got proof?" he said.

"I can't tell Mom," she said. "You know how she can be sometimes—so sheltered. I'm afraid she'd lose it." When she crossed her arms across her chest, he wanted to tell her a woman her age ought to be wearing a bra. "You're the one who always screamed and hollered, but she's the one I don't want to hurt."

Bite your tongue.

"It'll kill her if all this falls through, won't it?"

"You mean what you said?" he said.

"What?"

"You'd kill this baby if you and Gabriel split?"

"I hate him," she said.

"Not the baby you don't hate."

"I hate *him* that much," she said. "I do. He lies, all the time."

Only so far a man of God could go. "You kill that kid," he pointed at her stomach. "That'll kill your mother."

She cocked her head in a way that made him want to slap her. Then, she stepped back and looked away. "Don't tell her, Dad," she told him. "Don't say anything about this—not here anyway. Maybe on your way home or something. And don't say anything to Gabe either—this is my problem."

"Did you hear what I said?" he asked.

A flick of the hair, cocky, the old Donna. "I got a history of miscarriages," she said, and then she pulled the bottom of the halter down with both hands. "I already had two. Things happen."

"You don't have a history of murder," he told her.

The temperature gauge on the barbecue rose fast enough to move the arrow visibly.

She pulled both her hands through her beautiful, dark bronze hair. "I just want you to know," she said, "maybe to warn you–"

"You be careful," he told her. And then, "Are we talking about next week here, or next year–"

"I don't know," she said, and then, for the first time, something broke and she turned away and watched Taylor pull a ton of dirt out of the flowerbed. "I can't take it–being lied to."

Bite your tongue–don't tell her how many times she's done it herself. He took another step back from the grill that felt like a bomb. Sarah would say she has to know she's loved. Sarah would say, "Let her know, Mart–just let her know you love her."

"You can come home, Donna," he told her. "You can always come home."

Smoke was starting to seep out of the sides of the barbecue. Inside, gobs of last summer's grease popped and sizzled.

She turned, angrily. "Even if I'm not pregnant?" she said.

"Why does the baby have to die?" he said.

Those hard eyes always scared him, so much tougher than he was—drugs, stealing a Walk-man, drunk and hung over, looking forever like death warmed over.

"Even if I'm not pregnant, Dad—can I come home?"

Fire started to drip out of the bottom of the Webber. He'd bit his tongue a dozen times already. But this was life, a baby. That's what she was talking about. There had to be limits, had to be. A child sacrificed because she can't take being lied to? Sarah's face rose like a roadblock, but he gunned the engine. "You're my daughter. You can always come home," he told her, "but you take that kid's life and I won't be there."

Blackness in her eyes. Darkness.

And then he said, "You, of all people—" he said, "adopted like you were."

Her face was a pool of ice. "You always thought you were God," she said, then turned and jerked Taylor's dirty hands from the rose patch, picked him up the way LBJ picked up hounds, and dragged him back to their apartment.

In the long story of Donna Fleet, she'd ripped him so often he couldn't begin to remember all the bad words. But that one was a new twist—her father thought he was God. That one felt like burning coals: You always thought you were God. You always thought you were God.

*

He held his tongue at supper, even though there were very few words at all around. Gabe hauled in a barrel of chicken from Kentucky Fried, and they sat around the table, the TV blaring.
The whole time, Sarah didn't say a word, as if she were angry. So just to put something up for grabs other than what filth spewed from that infernal tube, he told them the story of the wedding he'd done back home, just before they left. How Rev. Vrieswyk, pushing eighty, a friend of the family, had stood up at the reception and thoroughly mixed up the names—Shannon was the bride and Mickey, her husband. How he kept mixing the names up, and how every last word he'd said—it was apropos, too, and well thought out—got lost completely because the families kept smirking at the old preacher's bumbling. He told that story as funny as he could, or tried to, and Gabe even laughed out loud.

"You game to go tomorrow morning?" Gabe asked him when Donna rose from the table and started throwing out paper plates.

"Game for what?" he said.

"Flea market, down at the track?" he said, smiling. "We got a ton of stuff."

"Tomorrow's Saturday," he said.

Gabe shrugged his shoulders. "Saturday, Sunday—don't matter."

Sunday doesn't matter, he told himself. "How early?" he said.

"Up with sun," Gabe said. "Got to get a place. This is one huge flea market."

"I won't sleep anyway," he said. "May as well make myself useful."

"It's something to do," Gabe said, pulling out a cigarette.

I could tell you something to do, Martin thought. *Starting tonight yet, I could tell you a whole lot to do—and what not, too.*

"I'm going to go box it, load it in the van," Gabe said, getting up from the table. "It'll take awhile. We ought to make a mint." Never once looked at his wife.

Sarah picked up the dishes and never said a thing other than the million prayers she was bringing to God in silence. He knew that because he knew his wife. He could see it in ner face, the fear. Makes you want to go home and hide in Minnesota snow, he thought.

But Donna was right—hearing the truth would break her mother's heart, so he told himself he wasn't about to tell her anything. Listen to Donna, he thought. Listen to her on this one because she's right. There will come a time on the trip back.

*

So he said nothing at all when he and Sarah were tucked in bed that night, in the master bedroom, where Donna insisted they'd sleep the whole time they'd be visiting. He didn't tell Sarah he'd seen the Minnesota nurse running her fingers through the angel Gabriel's hair, didn't tell her Donna had given him every reason to believe that sooner than they might guess she'd be parked on their doorstep once again. Didn't say a thing, except one question, the one that punished him all during the meal, ever since Donna had said it. "Sarah," he said, as they were lying there, "do you believe that sometimes I think of myself as God?"

Sarah wasn't at all surprised. "She told you that, didn't she?"

"How did you know?"

"She told me when she came back this afternoon." And then, "What'd you two talk about? You told her, didn't you? —You can't keep your mouth shut. You went and told her what you think is going on—"

"I did not," he said. "I swear."

She rolled over on her side, away from him.

"I didn't say a word."

"Then what did you talk about?"

He'd long ago assumed the Lord would look past a fairly long list of white lies. "I said I'd appreciate it if I heard *her* pray once in a while," he told her. It was true—not that he'd told her that, but that he felt that way.

"That's all?"

"And I told her she shouldn't handle Taylor so rough or he'd grow up to regret it—"

"Oh, Mart," she said.

"Isn't it true?"

"Well, yes, of course—but haven't we been all through this?"

"Well, then, is it true what your daughter said?" he asked. "She thinks I think I'm God—is that the way I come off, the way I've been for all these years?"

"I don't want to answer that question right now," she said.

He waited for silence to cover up tracks. "It's not good, Sarah," he told her.

Nothing.

A purplish glow filled the room from the lava lamp on the bureau. He turned away from her and watched round forms elongate and break into balls of ooze.

"You heard me," he said. "And you know, too."

"Don't go riding in there and try to make it all right," she said. "Just stay out, okay?"

Just outside the door he heard Letterman on TV. Donna was alone on the couch. They'd stayed with the kids for a long time when she'd said she wanted to help Gabe box up the booty, but now the kids were in bed in their tiny room, Gabe still loading the van, hours after he'd left. Donna was alone out there, waiting, probably, for what might never come—if not tonight, then some other for sure.

Still, it was this God business that haunted him. He remembered reading a line years ago—"there's the work and there's the man." Maybe you get only one calling in life—father or preacher or landscaper or dairyman—only one role you can fill well, and maybe he'd spent too much of his time preaching the Word and not enough being the loving father he should have been. Not five years ago, Mrs. Bakker had told him how her son—he couldn't remember the kid's name—had announced one Sunday dinner that God had a cold, when all he'd meant was the preacher, the man whose voice he'd heard from the pulpit.

His daughter was thirty years old, but maybe she'd always carried the same view, maybe because she was right. He'd never considered himself the almighty God, the everlasting Father, Prince of Peace, never designed to become the immortal, invisible, God over all. Or did he? Often enough, he'd thought of himself as God's hands in a weary world—at a funeral, at a deathbed. In times of pain and sorrow, he carried the Word into the fray. He'd played the prophet Nathan, creating stories to snare a sinners like David. It was his calling to minister.

Maybe he'd done it wrong. What did he know—the son of a preacher himself? He remembered nights his mother used to shush him, only because his father was writing a sermon, reading the Word. He'd respected his father, always respected him—maybe respect wasn't enough.

Up there on the shelf the digital alarm flicked stick-like numbers he watched and waited to change. He'd always disliked digitals because a clock made life seem a process, a sweep; but maybe digitals were better. There are separate moments, after all, moments when everything changes. Maybe he was at one.

If I've ever once thought myself like you, Lord, he said, *forgive me. If I've lied to myself, too cock sure that what I was up to was your will, then wash me now, whiter than snow.*

Something reached up in his chest and pulled his face tight. Maybe Donna was right. Something stiff and unyielding melted in his chest and arms and legs. Something bitter as bile dripped from his soul–he could feel it. The old man had to die before something new could be rise from the darkness.

He had to get out of that bed and tell his daughter, tell Donna how sorry he was. He had to stand there and tell her that if ever in his life he came off as God he was dead wrong. *Forgive me*, he said to the Lord, *when I thought of myself too highly*–because it had to have happened sometime. *When I did, Lord, forgive me. Not* if *I did, but when I did–wipe it all away.*

He swept his hand through his hair, buttoned up his pajama top, and stepped outside.

"I'm sorry," he told Donna. He'd closed the door behind him so Sarah didn't have to hear it. "I'm sorry, honey," he told his daughter. "I'm really sorry if I ever gave you cause to believe that I think I'm God."

Donna sat there on the couch, her hair pinned up behind her head, her bare feet sticking out from her pajamas. The darkness was gone from her eyes and washed from her face by streams of cry lines. She pointed the remote at the TV and clicked it off.

"I should have known," he told her. "If anybody should, I should have known I was coming off that way."

She could barely raise her eyes. "Come sit here," she said. "Come sit here beside me, Daddy." She patted the afghan. "Don't apologize, okay?"

He took three steps around the long coffee table and sat down. He raised his arm around her, pulled her shoulder close, took her hand. *How many times had he ever done that?* he asked himself. *Praise God.* She snuggled in.

But she was crying, the girl was crying. "This is what it's been like," she said, "for too many nights—just me in this dump. Do you understand? This is what it's been like, and I know what he's up to—I just know it. Do you realize what that's like?"

"He's boxing stuff up," Martin said. "He's getting ready for the flea market."

"That's a lie," she told him. "That's just another lie."

The number came back to him. *256*, he could have said. *I know for a fact e's in 256.*

"I didn't think it would happen with you here," she told him, through her teeth—that angry. "I thought maybe while you were visiting, he'd stick around. He'd at least make it look good." She shook her head. "I got all geared up for your coming for just that reason—I thought maybe things would go better." She put her head on his chest. "I didn't think he'd pull this shit, Dad. I didn't think he'd have the balls to go on with it when you around." He felt her hand on his, clutching. "But he doesn't give a damn who he hurts." And then she looked at him. "How much, Dad?"

"What do you mean?"

"How much can you take?"

He felt her stomach beneath his hand. "It's not me you got to think about," he said. "I don't mean nothing at all. It's not what I can take that matters."

"Don't give me preacher answers," she said.

"I'm not."

"You are too," she told him, loosening her grip.

He leaned back and took his beautiful daughter softly at the nape of her neck, rubbed her lightly with his fingers. "This is the whole truth, Donna, and you already know it: nothing we do has to count forever. That's what the Lord says. You know that."

Things came haltingly. Her arms were tense as cables. "I did stuff that would make you and Mom puke," she told him. "You don't know the half of it. I'm tired of it, Dad. I'm tired and I'm sick—"

"You can always come home," he said.

She raised her face slightly. "No matter what?" she said.

"No matter what," he told her.

"And you're going to be there?" she said.

"I'm going to be there," he told her. "I swear it."

He pulled her into his arms, pulled her so close he felt her chest heave when she started to cry. "I don't know what to do, Dad," she told him. "You don't know what I've done."

With a descent that didn't shock him, tumbling as it did to the level of the most hideous, his mind showed him a vision as clear as any he'd ever seen—the angel Gabriel sprawled out somewhere in the storage room, perfectly dead in the middle of all that booty. Something in him reached a point he knew all too well hers could have or might.

Good Lord, he said to himself. Good, good Lord. He sat on the couch with his beautiful daughter crying in his arms, her tears wet against his neck, her arms around his chest, her clean hands holding him in a way she'd never done before; and all the while he sat there he was praying like a saint, a thousand petitions in the voice of his soul's groaning.

But to her, to his precious daughter, he was saying nothing at all. Nothing.

He is like a tree planted by streams of water, which yields fruit in season and whose leaf does not wither.
Psalm 1:3